ONE MUST SURVIVE

When an unmarked fighter with her guns blazing came screaming out of the sun, the pilot of the peaceful airliner en route for Hanoi had no chance of avoiding the murderous fire. The airliner crashed into the trackless wastes of Burma. Amazingly, eleven people survived, and with them was a dying man who told of a fantastic plot to destroy the American bomber base on the tropical islands of Nakai. One of the eleven had to get back to civilisation to stop the holocaust . . .

ROBERT CHARLES

ONE MUST SURVIVE

Complete and Unabridged

LINFORD
Leicester

First published in Great Britain

First Linford Edition
published 1998

British Library CIP Data

Charles, Robert, *1938* –
    One must survive.—Large print ed.—
Linford mystery library
    1. Detective and mystery stories
    2. Large type books
    I. Title
    823.9'14 [F]

    ISBN 0–7089–5347–6

Published by
F. A. Thorpe (Publishing) Ltd.
Anstey, Leicestershire

Set by Words & Graphics Ltd.
Anstey, Leicestershire
Printed and bound in Great Britain by
T. J. International Ltd., Padstow, Cornwall

This book is printed on acid-free paper

1

Sky Pirate

Steve Navarr was in his usual mood, sour and cynical. A tall man and well built, he was leaning idly in the open doorway to the main passenger lounge at Nakai airport. His eyes took in the sweating assortment of humanity that sprawled, talking or drinking, around the room. They were a mixed lot, and only one of them had the energy to stand, a dark wary-eyed man whom Navarr guessed to be French. He stood alone by the bar and his nervous stance showed that he was tense and afraid.

Navarr knew that there was a story behind the lone Frenchman, a newspaperman's instinct told him that. But he wasn't interested. Had their paths crossed ten years ago Navarr might well have been buying the man a drink by now, and tactfully worming the story out

1

of him. However, a lot had changed in ten years. Navarr had made the grade as a foreign correspondent for the giant Trans-Continental News Agency. Now he waited to be given big assignments, rather than hunt the small ones down.

Abruptly a babble of voices broke out behind him.

'Why?' A woman's voice was demanding haughtily. 'Why the devil should I go to Hanoi when I want to get to Manila?'

'But, Miss Valoise, I have explained — '

'I don't want explanations. I want a plane to Manila.'

'But, Lorretta, darling — '

'And will you stop all this Lorretta darling stuff. I don't want it. All I want is a plane to take me to Manila.'

'But we have no planes for charter. And no scheduled flights — '

'Well, change the schedule.'

'But, Lorretta, darling, they can't. And it will only mean a few more flying hours to go via Hanoi and Hong Kong.'

'I *do not* want to go to Hanoi. I *do not* want to go to Hong Kong. And I most definitely *do not* want any more extra flying hours. I'm fed up with flying.'

Navarr turned slowly, long after the other occupants of the lounge had fixed their gaze upon the small party which was causing all the commotion. The complaining woman in the centre of the group was of the type that always brought a cynical smile to Navarr's lips. Physically she was beautiful. Her rich blonde hair fell in a shoulder-length wave that curved forwards on each side to frame her face. Her figure was perfect, the hips neatly curved and her full breasts only just hidden by a deeply cleft blouse of yellow silk. Her pale blue costume had been tailored by an expert, and the legs beneath the tight-fitting skirt were sheathed in golden-tinged nylon stockings. To look at, she was ravishing and she knew it; and because of it she was making hell of the lives of the men around her. At the moment she had half a dozen frustrated males vainly trying to soothe her as she poured out a torrent of haughty complaints.

Navarr watched the proceedings with amusement. Two or three harassed airport officials were repeatedly insisting that they could not rearrange all their flight schedules merely to fly her direct to Manila, while a balding little man in spectacles tried hopelessly to prevent her from continuing the scene. The little man was addressing her as 'Lorretta darling' with every breath, and was sweating profusely.

Navarr came to the conclusion that, if he had to handle 'Lorretta darling', he would do so by stretching her across his knee and thoroughly flaying the seat of her skirt. After that it was possible that she might develop into a normal, likeable woman. He began to hope that one of the men would do just that, but none of them did. It was a pity, he thought, it would have done them all a lot of good.

'Oh, damn it all!' said the blonde suddenly. 'And damn you, too, Barney! As a manager you'd make a helluva fine dishwasher.'

She broke away and made for the lounge, while the little man, who was obviously Barney, gaped after her like a horrified fish which had just been skewered.

Practically a dozen paces separated the blonde from the door where Navarr stood. She gave him a blue-eyed glare that would have sent an impressionable man scurrying out of her way. But Steve Navarr was not easily impressed. He stood in the centre of the doorway with both hands in his pockets, meeting her glare with a half-smile.

There was room for her to pass on either side but she walked straight at him. Only at the last minute did she hesitate and stop.

Navarr said amiably: 'Careful, honey, your temper is showing.'

The blonde drew an angry breath, a scathing retort already forming on her lips. Navarr glanced down, the surge of her breasts was enough to attract any man's eyes, and there was enough of them showing to make most men hop aside in embarrassment. Only Navarr wasn't easily embarrassed either.

The blonde hesitated without speaking, something warning her that this was one man who wouldn't dance to her tune. She flung her head back haughtily and stepped around him. As she went she flung back petulantly:

'Some people just haven't *any* manners.'

Navarr smiled and idly stepped aside as Barney dashed after her with a nervous apology. A resigned-looking young man followed him at a slower pace, while the airport officials wisely disbanded in different directions. Navarr turned to face the lounge, his hands still deep in the pockets of his pale grey suit. 'Lorretta darling' had parked herself in an armchair, and, despite her rage, she had possessed the forethought to display her figure in the best possible lounging pose. It was then that Navarr recognised her.

It was the pose that did it. The shoulders well back to emphasise the swelling curves beneath her blouse, the silken gold wave of her hair falling forward over her right shoulder, and the shapely legs neatly crossed to expose a tantalising glimpse of velvet-smooth, stockinged thigh. Navarr had seen that pose several times in magazines, and in films at cinemas. Her name was Lorretta de Valoise, and she was latest in the long line of aspiring screen blondes. From the little that he occasionally read in the showtime gossip columns he judged her to be something between a starlet and a star. He watched her starting into another temperamental scene and decided that maybe Flight Eighteen would make an interesting trip to Hanoi.

* * *

In the crew room the crew of Flight Eighteen was preparing to leave. Rayburn and Kelley, the pilot and co-pilot, were making a last-minute check of the flight plan with Navigator Hatch Connors. Behind them Wallis, the radio operator, was leaning over the dark-haired, merry-eyed Kay Leonard. The air hostess looked the very essence of neat efficiency in her smart blue uniform. Her cheeks were flushed with a smile and her lustrous hazel eyes were sparkling.

'How about it?' Wallis was saying. 'Dump those two perishing reprobates and let a gentleman buy you a dinner. I know the best spot in all Hanoi for wine and music. It's got the best cabaret in town and the lights are always low. What do you say?'

'What he means is that it's pitch dark in the corners and the cabaret girls dance in the altogether,' Scott Kelley interrupted warmly.

'This is a decent place,' Wallis grinned. 'One *you* wouldn't know about.'

Rayburn and Connors joined them. 'Children,' Rayburn said carefully, he always addressed them in the same way. 'Children, I have a suggestion. I propose that we request three more hostesses from the company, then we'll have enough to go round.'

Unanimous assent greeted his remark, supported by Kay, who remarked that it was one way in which she might achieve a little peace and quiet. Connors, who had earned his first name from the number of glasses he had emptied 'down the hatch' promptly demanded that they drink to it.

While the others lectured the navigator

on the subject of temperance, the fair-haired, almost boyish-looking, Scott Kelley sat down on the edge of Kay's chair. 'You see what kind of company you're in, Kay? Hatch is a drunk who will undoubtedly finish up on skid row. Wallis is already on the wanted list of every vice squad in South East Asia. And poor old Rayburn is old enough to be your daddy. In fact, knowing Rayburn, it's quite possible that he is. That just leaves me. I'm the only one fit enough to — '

He had to duck sharply to avoid a cushion hurled by Wallis, and he promptly retreated behind Kay's chair. Connors seized a springy ruler from the desk and followed Wallis into action.

'Pack it up you two.' Kelley instructed hopefully. 'Or you can buy your own beer in Hanoi.'

Kay Leonard jumped between them. 'All right, boys, all of you quieten down. If our passengers were to hear the way you play about the company would go out of business. Nobody would trust themselves in the air with you.'

Jim Rayburn grinned, and added his own weight to her entreaty for peace. Rayburn had been a pilot for a long time, but he had never before flown with a crew like this one. Despite their larking about on the ground, in the air, they were still the best crew the company possessed.

Rayburn himself was nearing fifty, a big man with thick grey hair and blue eyes. For thirty years he had been flying, mostly over the Asiatic routes. He reckoned he knew every bar and night club in every airport in Asia, and yet, despite that, he drank very little. He just liked the atmosphere and the good times, and — woe betide him if his wife ever found out — the stage shows and cabarets where smooth-skinned girls performed eastern dances in nothing more concealing than a glistening film of sweat.

He listened now to the banter between the three younger men and the girl. Wallis, he knew, was merely stirring it for the other two. The radio operator had a girl back in England whom he was due to marry as soon as he could reasonably afford it. Still he liked to make things just a little harder for the two rivals who had been pursuing Kay Leonard ever since they had first clapped eyes on her. Not for the first time Rayburn wondered how it would eventually turn out. One of those two would have to be best man at the wedding and he wasn't sure that either of them could take it.

He glanced down at his watch and realised that it was time they left. 'Come on, children,' he ordered. 'We've got a plane to fly to Hanoi.'

Promptly they collected up their flight plans and passenger lists, checked that their caps were straight, and once again became calm, efficient servants of the airline.

★ ★ ★

Steve Navarr had by now raised sufficient energy to cross over to the bar, something that, in this strength-sapping heat, he considered a minor feat of achievement. Glass in hand, he was calmly watching the chair where Lorretta de Valoise was still holding her pose, even though her

11

shoulders must have been aching with the strain. Once or twice she shot acid looks at him which conveyed the impression that she would be highly pleased if he were to fall dead on the spot. The thought amused him, and he enjoyed the remainder of his drink all the better for it. Ordering a second, he began idly to review the events that had brought him to Nakai.

Nakai was the largest of a small group of islands in the shimmering blue of the Bay of Bengal. Situated a hundred and twenty miles off the east coast of India and approximately four hundred miles north of the island of Ceylon, the group had remained for centuries an interesting sprinkle of dots on the map. On the large scale maps that is, on most maps it was not even marked.

The islands, there were four of them and a scattering of rocky outcrops, were independent and self-governed. The inhabitants, numbering four to five thousand fishermen and farmers, were of mixed Indian and Sinhalese descent. Civilisation had almost overlooked this lonely outpost, and barely a tenth of the inhabitants had received any education. The members of the governing council were quite competent in looking after their own affairs, but were almost totally ignorant of the world outside. This leisurely state of uncivilised innocence might have lasted indefinitely but for one thing. For over three hundred years time had passed the Nakai islands by; no one had bothered them, for there was nothing to make them worth while bothering about. Then, abruptly, the United States Air Force had realised that the wide flat plain on the north side of Nakai would make an ideal air base, and from then on the onslaught of civilisation had hammered the bewildered population into awed stupor. The unsuspecting government had been easily talked into sanctioning the construction of the air base and within a matter of weeks work on the great runways had begun. Living quarters were going up, shops, hospitals, cinemas, and even bowling alleys, began to grow. The get-rich-quick merchants moved in, and bars and night clubs sprang up. And for the first time Nakai realised exactly what it had let itself in for and began to doubt.

Now the air base had been built and the heavy nuclear bombers were coming in. With them came the American servicemen and their families. They brought ice-boxes and TV sets, and great gleaming cars. There was nowhere to drive to and no roads to drive on, but they still brought their cars. Roads, they told each other, were something they were gonna have to build.

The natives of Nakai watched dubiously. The chewing gum and the Coca Cola and the whisky that the strangers brought were all very well, but as for the rest they were not sure that they liked it. But the troubles of Nakai were only just beginning. Left to themselves the majority of the islanders would no doubt have eventually resigned themselves to being civilised. Civilisation had happened almost everywhere else and in time they too, would have accepted it. But there were some who would not let them accept it, strangers of their own kind, who stirred dark rumours about their future. Strangers who warned them against the folly of exposing themselves to dangers they did not understand.

It was soon obvious that communist agitators were stirring up the islanders. Of the few educated sections of the population the majority were pro-communist. They had been against their government from the start, and with the help of skilled *agent provocateurs* were finding it easy to play on the simple minds of the people. They incited riots and aroused high tension on the island, and soon Nakai became another world trouble spot. And Steve Navarr had found himself once more on a special assignment for Trans-Continental.

During the last week or two there had been some ugly incidents between the resident islanders and the scores of Indian workers whom the Americans had brought over from India. The island had simmered like a pot on the boil, at intervals bubbling over into violence. The communists had done their work well and pin-pointed the trouble spot as a world-wide controversy. And although nobody doubted the fact, there was no proof that it was their doing.

The clear tones of a girl announcer on the loudspeaker brought Navarr away from his thoughts. Flight Eighteen for Hanoi was almost due to leave, and passengers were advised to take their seats. Navarr emptied his glass and crossed the lounge to the bags he had left by the door, a small suitcase and a portable typewriter in a leather case. Navarr always travelled light.

He followed the other passengers out to the plane that was waiting on the tarmac outside.

The smiling Kay Leonard ticked off their names as they went up the gangway, and Navarr decided that here was a girl who was more his type than the temperamental Lorretta. He liked the relaxed, friendly, way she smiled, and found himself wishing he knew how to react to a girl like that. He entered the plane, thinking that if he tried anything he would most probably offend her. On the rare occasions when he had tried to approach an exceptionally pretty girl with the usual ulterior motives he had gone about it clumsily and offended her, so now it seemed safer not to try.

He sat down in his seat and idly speculated on the story he had been sent to get. He was lean-faced, which was somewhat surprising when one considered his well-built body. His eyes were an alert brown, and his hair black and very slightly waved. He was a hard-lipped man who accepted few favours and offered fewer, a lone wolf in a cynical shell, the type that in fiction most women would want to mother or befriend, their sympathies aroused to tenderness. Only in real life no one was ever sorry for Navarr — except on rare and totally-drunk occasions, Navarr himself.

He was still speculating on Nakai, and the air base that was now an important link in the chain of defence posts that faced Moscow, when a second passenger plumped down beside him.

'Excuse please,' the newcomer said deferentially. 'Is very hot, isn't it? Very hot?'

Navarr studied his companion as he sat down. He saw a shortish man, portly and round-faced. He wore an off-white linen suit and somehow managed to bear a collar and a yellow tie. He wore glasses, and his thinning hair looked as though it might have been painted on his scalp with a lightly bristled paint-brush. Sitting down he wiped his face with an initialled handkerchief, the letter W woven in red silk in one corner.

'Hot,' he said again. 'Very hot.'

'One could almost say exceptionally hot,' Navarr agreed blankly.

'Quite so, yes.'

'Or possibly excessively hot, but definitely hot.'

'Yes, yes, very hot,' rejoined the other.

Navarr almost laughed aloud at the little man's bland answer. For once his sarcasm was being wasted.

The little man mopped his face again. 'Very very hot,' he repeated. He looked at Navarr and beamed.

'My name is Schelde. Wilhem Schelde. I am from Brussels. I am pleased to meet you.'

'Steve Navarr.' The tall cynic accepted the hand that was offered to him with a flicker of amusement. There was something very likeable about Schelde.

In the seats opposite them the eye-catching Lorretta de Valoise was deciding upon which pose to adopt, while the weary-looking Barney collapsed against the window. The young man travelling with them slumped down in the seat behind with an expression that could only have been caused by a king-sized headache. Lorretta finally settled on a lounging pose with her head well back to reveal her profile. The sight seemed to entrance Schelde, but it brought only a smile from Navarr.

A few seats ahead, the man whom Navarr had rightly guessed to be French was buckling himself into his seat. There was a half smile about his mouth now, and if anyone could have read his thoughts they would have known why, for he had never expected to get out of Nakai alive.

At the head of the gangway Kay Leonard checked off the last of the passengers. There was a flashy American who answered to the name of Leo Rex, who gave her a look that ought to have earned him a slap in the face, an elderly English couple named Ballard who looked a little bewildered by all the activity; a few Chinese and an Indian, and then a little moon-faced woman in a green sarong. Last there came a dark-faced man with almost sinister looks. His close cropped hair was a scrubby carpet of short black curls and his cheeks were badly pock-marked. Kay knew from the list in her hand that he was Greek and answered to the name of Nico Dorapho.

Soon the plane was moving out on to the runway, gathering speed, and finally lifting into the perfect sky. The small airfield and its few buildings fell away, and then, as the plane rose above the jungle-coated mountains that reared up from the centre of the island, they saw the sprawling bomber base that the U.S. Air Force had built on the other side. The great and grimly beautiful aircraft below glinted in the harsh sunlight and the white glare of the runways shimmered like sheets of water in the heat haze. Gradually the green mountains and slashing ravines and gorges of central Nakai faded behind them, dwindling into a dark green bulge like a crooked elbow jutting out of the sea. The smaller islands were visible for a little while, but soon the whole group had vanished into the unbelieveable blue of the Bay of Bengal, a blue horizon that scintillated with dancing spangles of silver in the sunlight.

Navarr watched the scene below until the dazzle became too much for his eyes and made him turn his gaze away. It was then that he became aware of Schelde talking by his side.

' . . . is beautiful,' the little Belgian was saying. 'The most beautiful city in the world. You must come to Brussels one day, Mr. Navarr, and see if I am not right. I have travelled many places in my life, but nowhere is there a city like my Brussels.'

'You're a native of Brussels then?'

Again the sarcasm was wasted.

'Yes,' said Schelde. 'Yes that is so.

I work for the Brestanile automobile factories. I arrange export orders abroad. Our cars are small saloons and more suitable for Nakai than the big American cars, so there is good business there. It is a good job, but it keeps me away so much from my own country . . . '

Navarr resigned himself with having to put up with the little man for the rest of the trip, and decided that maybe he wasn't so likeable after all. He was too talkative. And he didn't need a partner, merely a listener.

On the flight deck, Big Jim Rayburn was humming to himself as he watched the blue seas pass below. He liked the feel of the controls in his hands and was never happier than when he was in the air. To him there was nothing better than a cruise in the clouds on a day like this, unless of course it was the ebony-skinned movements of the cabaret girls he loved to watch.

Four hours passed. The airliner was not a jet and far from new, but it maintained a steady two hundred and thirty m.p.h. until almost a thousand miles of sea gave way to the green and rolling coastline of Burma. The foamy ribbon of white lace that fringed the sand rippled in the sunlight, receding in shallow swirls to the blue of the sea. Then it was gone, and they flew inland over the jungle-shrouded hills and ravines. The earth was a vast sea of green ridges, like wild high waves whipped up in the silent rage of an invisible storm. The airliner's shadow dipped and rose through the wooded ranges, cruising smoothly on, regardless of the terrain.

Beside Rayburn, Scott Kelley was idly thinking of the night life of Hanoi, and the smiling face that dominated his dreams was the face of Kay Leonard. Occasionally Hatch Connors would enter his thoughts and he would feel vaguely uncomfortable. Kay seemed to take an equal delight in the company of either one of them, and Scott would have given a lot to have Hatch find another girl. The two men had flown together for over a year now, forming a happy-go-lucky friendship that had been sealed in a toast of beer and maintained by frequently painting the town a fiendish scarlet. Now they had a problem, and another girl for Hatch would settle it nicely. He realised ruefully that Hatch probably harboured the same thoughts in reverse.

Abruptly Kelley did what he always did when he found his thoughts getting too serious. He stopped thinking. Time would work it out somehow. He turned his attention to the scenery again, and realised that they were flying high over a series of rugged, forested mountains. In places knuckled fists of rock and crag pushed through the green blanket, and once a glittering sliver of blue marked the twisted, downward course of a stream. The scene was instilled with a sinister kind of beauty, the wooded flanks of the ranges hiding a treacherous terrain with a bright cloak of velvet green. Kelley watched the heights pass beneath, and start to give way to lower hills, endless parallel ridges, like green furrows churned by a giant plough.

Then suddenly:

'What the hell?'

Kelley turned as Big Jim Rayburn ejaculated the words in an angry yell. He saw the pilot's blue eyes widen with alarm and automatically followed their gaze.

The sun blinded him, and for seconds he couldn't see. Then he picked up a streak of silver that was flashing out of the sun. He felt the plane lurch as Rayburn put her into an instinctive roll, and in the same second he saw the orange flashes spearing out of the wings of the oncoming fighter as she opened fire.

She's attacking, he thought stupidly. That bloody crazy sky pirate wants to shoot us down!

The staccato snarl of tracer bullets filled his ears as the slim fighter came screaming in for the kill.

2

Shot Down

Jim Rayburn felt the crippling hammer blow of a hit as the pirate fighter swooped in and raked the defenceless airliner with a burst of tracer fire. It slammed him back in his seat with vicious force and seemed to rip his entire stomach apart. He felt the blood spill out and run down between his thighs as he fought to pull the plane out of the rolling dive. His insides were a burning furnace of agonised pain and the whole cabin was revolving crazily through a blood-red haze. Somehow he hung his weight on the stick and the plane became level. Then the pirate killer dived in again.

There were no identification markings on the mystery fighter. She came hurtling out of the sun after a fast climbing turn, her wing guns streaming fire. The shuddering impact ripped up the length of the stricken plane as she wallowed through the sky. Smoke gushed from the airliner's engines, thick swirling clouds that were suddenly split by leaping spearheads of red flame. The spearheads swelled and roared, and then erupted into flailing sheets of scarlet fire.

Rayburn saw the engines flaming through the red veil, and bit clean through his lower lip as he strained to put the airliner into another dive. Like a flaming arrow she screamed down towards the jungle hills.

The sky pirate wheeled once through the sky as her victim made the death plunge. Then she turned and flew northwards at full speed.

Rayburn watched her go. His body was racked with pain, and the blood had formed a large sticky pool on the chair between his legs. But still one fighting part of his brain was concentrating on the fighter. He had to wait for her to leave before he could attempt to pull the airliner out of her dive and try for a crash landing. Through the red veil that was streaming blood from a lacerated scalp he watched the sky pirate speed away. Then he hung his dying frame on the stick and tried to pull her out of her death dive.

He couldn't do it.

He fought to get the stick back with all the remnants of his fading strength, but already his life had almost ebbed away in the red stream that ran down his torn stomach. He just couldn't do it.

Then a new hand closed on the stick. Scott Kelley came out of a black-out on a wave of agony from his right arm, which had been shattered from shoulder to elbow. He saw the ghastly wreck, that had been his pilot and friend, fighting a losing battle to bring the plane up, and he reached across to get a grip on the stick with his left hand. He half turned in his seat, facing the rear of the plane to get more pull on the stick. Together he and the pilot strained, and the airliner's nose came up. Kelley heaved with all his strength to get the stick moving, but it was Rayburn's great weight that really did it. The plane straightened, but lost speed as she hurtled along just above tree-top level.

Rayburn was hardly aware that Kelley was helping him as he watched the tree tops flashing underneath them. He was numb now, his lower limbs and stomach were dead, and death was reaching up to stop his great heart. But somehow that heart kept beating; not until the actual impact as they crashed down did Rayburn intend to die.

A low valley came up, a valley flanked with thick jungle but choked with only lighter growth at the bottom. It looked as though a stream had once run there, and the bed was now over-grown with vegetation. Rayburn knew he had no time to find a better place, and with the last of his strength he pushed at the stick. The plane's nose dipped as she swooped in, and in the same moment death triumphed as Big Jim Rayburn slumped over the controls.

Scott Kelley saw the valley bottom rushing beneath them and flung up his good arm to protect his face as they crashed. The airliner ploughed into the dense vegetation with a sickening impact that hurled him forwards against the straps of his harness and like a screaming engine of destruction careered along the valley floor, tearing bushes and ferns and shrubs asunder. It slewed round and one wing snapped off like a brittle twig. Then the jungle wall reared up and the plane hit it with a shuddering crash. Kelley saw a wall of greenery smash down at him, but by a miracle the cockpit glass didn't break. Vines and branches slashed across it but somehow it held. The broken airliner seemed to vibrate like a thing of living flesh in its death throes. Then, with a final quiver, she relapsed into stillness.

Sound took over, the dull snarl and crackle of burning.

Kelley roused himself with an effort. With pain tearing at his nerves he struggled to undo his harness with one hand. He succeeded and then made an attempt to rouse Rayburn. Even as he tried he knew that Rayburn with his ripped-open stomach and blood-smeared face could not possibly be alive. But he had to try. He felt suddenly sick, and then nausea dragged him down into a twisted heap beside the dead pilot.

Hatch Connors picked himself up slowly from the floor. The fire from the killer fighter had missed him, and only the savage battering he had taken as the plane crashed had put him down. By rights he should have been a mess of bloodied pulp, yet somehow nothing seemed to be broken. He swayed like a drunk on the floor, and then he saw Wallis.

The cheerful radio operator hung like a broken puppet in his seat. Tracer fire had riddled his chest like a sieve and wiped half of his face away. Connors turned aside, fighting down an urge to be sick. He saw the bloodied figure of Rayburn and realised that the pilot too was dead. Only Kelley was alive, heaving and retching in a heap on the floor. Connors grabbed the co-pilot beneath the shoulders and hauled him clear. Kelley moaned with pain and passed out. With an effort Connors got his friend on his shoulder and staggered towards the rear of the plane.

Back in the passenger cabin the tracer fire from the mystery fighter had created almost as much havoc. Half the passengers were dead or dying. As the plane swooped down Kay Leonard had yelled at them all to fasten their belts and most of those who were still alive had done so. Kay herself had followed her own advice for there was nothing else she could do for the passengers.

Steve Navarr was one of those who had escaped the tracer fire and belted himself in. When the airliner hit, something had caught him a savage crack above the left ear and he had blacked out. He came round to find Schelde trying to rouse him by repeatedly slapping his face. Somewhere ahead a woman was screaming and behind him he could hear the voice of the air hostess shouting.

'Wake up, Navarr, wake up!' Schelde seemed almost hysterical, as Navarr struggled upright and fumbled with his belt.

'All right, all right!' He managed to get out, as he unbuckled the straps.

Behind them Kay Leonard had already reached the door and was struggling with the clamps. She was sweating and frightened, blood was smearing the side of her white throat and her ribs hurt like fury where she had been flung from one side to the other.

'Easy, Miss, take it easy now.'

She recognised the dark-skinned Greek as he came up behind her and took over the job of unfastening the clamps. There was a half smile on his pock-marked face and he no longer looked sinister. Between them they got the doors open.

Kay turned to face the inside of the plane as the cooling draught of hot air rushed through the opening.

'Everybody out,' she called. Her voice was so unexpectedly calm that it practically startled her. 'Don't panic, just take your turn and leave the plane.' She glanced at the Greek. 'You'd better go first, you can help them down.'

Dorapho grinned and hooked one arm around her waist. 'Ladies first,' he ordered, and swinging her through the open door he dropped her on to the green cushion of vegetation.

'Hurry up now,' he called into the plane. 'Get a bloody move on in there.'

33

The American staggered past him as he spoke, and then he moved farther into the plane to grab at a pair of frightened Chinese and hustle them on.

Farther up the plane Navarr and Schelde were gaining their feet. Schelde slipped on a pool of blood and then hurried towards the back of the plane. Navarr saw the blonde actress hanging limp but alive in her seat. Beside her the little Barney had apparently failed to fasten his belt and had been shot half into the seat in front. His neck was twisted and broken. The resigned young man behind them was bleeding at the mouth and stone dead.

Navarr made for the actress and unbuckled the belt around her waist. She came to as he pulled her upright, and even then he detected a trace of resentment in her eyes. He half-pushed, half-carried her towards the entrance, and saw the Greek coming to give him a hand.

'Get outside,' Dorapho panted. 'I'll hand her to you.'

'I'm okay,' Lorretta said weakly.

Navarr took her at her word and

34

dropped her bodily through the open doorway. Schelde suddenly bumped into him carrying a half-conscious woman and jumped boldly through the door.

For a moment Navarr and the Greek paused as they saw Connors come staggering down the aisle with the injured Kelley on his back.

'Are there any more?' Navarr rapped.

'All dead,' Connors said flatly. With the Greek's help he got Kelley out of the plane.

Navarr glanced round the shambles of the wrecked airliner, and heard the roaring of the fire up front. He saw the little oriental woman in the green sarong hanging dead in her straps. The shot body of an Indian slumped in another seat. The glazed eyes of the little man called Barney looked reproachful even in death. There was no one else alive. Over a dozen passengers sprawled like rag dolls about the burning airliner.

'Come out!' Hatch Connors bellowed as he saw the lone man still standing in the plane. 'The tanks will go up any minute.'

Navarr turned to get out and then he heard a moan. It came from the dark Frenchman whom he had believed to be dead in his seat. The man stirred, his chest was soaked with red but at least he was alive. Navarr tore away the straps that held the body and lifted the half-conscious man in his arms. He ran to the open door and saw Connors and the Greek waiting below. They took the Frenchman from him and he jumped down into the waist-high undergrowth. Between them they struggled through the tangled vegetation with the limp body held aloft, fighting their way to a small clearing where the others had already gathered.

They reached the clearing and lowered the body beside the limp form of a Chinese. The Chinaman looked as though he was already dead. Navarr turned to face the plane and in that moment the fuel tanks erupted with a deafening roar.

A rush of scarlet flame sheeted up and the heat hit them like a physical blow. The leaping tongues engulfed the nose of the stricken plane, swirling around it like gleeful, flickering little demons. Thick black smoke clouds billowed up and the acrid stench of burning filled the clear air. Snarling and crackling the fire-demons gorged on their fallen prey, dancing wildly through the smoke. The lush green vegetation that had cushioned the crashing plane writhed in the fiendish heat that charred it to ashes. The sound of the holocaust swelled to a giant rumble, as the funeral pyre of those still inside blazed up to the brassy blue of the Asian sky.

Scott Kelley recovered consciousness to feel the heat of the blazing plane on his face. He thought of Rayburn and felt a sense of shock. He began to tremble violently as he watched the blaze leap higher through the thick smoke and then a cool hand touched his face. He realised abruptly that his head was cushioned on something soft and looked up. Kay Leonard was kneeling with his head in her lap. Her cap was awry and her dark hair was tousled and flung forwards over her face. Her eyes were no longer merry and there was a trickle of red streaking the line of her throat where she had been nicked by a sliver of flying glass.

She felt the movement of his head and with it a surge of relief. 'Stay quiet, Scott,' she said, and her hand smoothed his cheek.

He looked around him and saw several of the passengers standing and staring at the burning airliner. Then he saw Connors. The light-hearted Navigator was standing with his fists clenched at his sides, his mouth was set tight and his eyes were wet with unshed tears.

'Where's Wall?' Kelley's voice was very weak.

Connors looked down.

'He bought it,' he said flatly.

Speaking seemed to ease the tension within him and he glanced around. The staring passengers were streaming sweat from the heat of the fire and he knew it was senseless to stay so close. A hundred yards down the valley he saw a clump of rocks on the jungle's edge and decided that that was his best objective.

'All right, everybody, start moving.' They looked round in faint surprise as he spoke and he went on. 'There's no point in standing here and roasting, we'll make for the shade of those rocks, there we can get away from this heat and out of the sun.'

He turned to Kelley. 'Can you manage, Scott?'

'I can manage.' Kelley spoke through clenched teeth and got to his feet with Kay Leonard's help.

'I'll look after him, Hatch,' the girl assured him.

Connors faced the others.

'Right. You men give me a hand with these two and we'll get going. A couple of you lead the way to break a trail and the body-bearers will bring up the rear.'

Dorapho gave a brief nod, and started kicking his way through the undergrowth towards the rock pile. The others picked up the senseless bodies of the Frenchman and the Chinese and followed him. Schelde, the little Belgian, was still helping the shock-dazed woman he had helped out of the plane.

The thick tangle of bush and ferns made the Greek's job a stiff one as he beat down a path along the valley floor. On their left the green barrier of the jungle wall brooded like a silent enemy, but the cool shadows beneath the twining vines looked very tempting. Dorapho began to soak in his own sweat.

It took them almost ten minutes to force their way through to the mound of lichen-covered boulders on the fringe of the jungle. Here, in the shade of the trees, the Greek and the two Chinese kicked a clear space for the others to lay down the two bodies. It was cooler in the shadows, and looking back they saw that the blaze had now died around their crashed airliner and the whole scene was shrouded in a thick curtain of oily black smoke.

Steve Navarr wiped the sweat out of his eyes as he helped to set the dark Frenchman down. As his hand came away he saw that his fingers were streaked with blood. His forehead was smarting and he realised that he must have broken the skin when the plane crashed. He leaned against one of the mossy boulders, and waited for the heave of his chest to steady down. He looked around the rest of the party slowly. They were a wild-looking crew to say the least, blood-smeared and smoke-streaked, their clothing blackened and burnt, their hair scuffed and awry. The only person whose hair still looked neat was Schelde, and that was only because the little man hadn't got a lot of hair to ruffle anyway.

Lorretta de Valoise was standing slightly apart from the others, her blonde waves were marred by black streaks and Navarr saw that her striking blue eyes were numbed with shock. Since he had thrown her out of the plane she had remained totally silent and now her full breasts were trembling with emotion.

'Barney,' she said at last. 'And Hal? Where are they?' Her voice was almost a whimper, strained and faltering.

Navarr realised that Hal must have been the resigned-looking young man who had been travelling with her. 'They're both dead,' he said evenly. 'They died when the plane hit down.'

Her mouth trembled and she turned

away. He expected her to burst into hysterics but she didn't. Her shoulders quivered a little and for a moment the hard-lipped cynic hesitated. If he had known the right words to say then it was possible that he would have said them. But he didn't know, and it was left to Connors to lay a friendly arm across her shoulders and help her to sit down on the nearest boulder. Navarr turned away.

The soft sound of sobbing reached his ears but he didn't look round, and it was a long time before he realised that it wasn't the actress who was crying. He did glance round then. Lorretta sat pale and dry-eyed on a rounded boulder, but beyond her the little Englishwoman whom Schelde had pulled out of the plane was crying bitterly. Navarr recalled that she had had a husband, one of the scattered and broken dolls which had littered the interior of the wrecked plane.

It was the crying of the Englishwoman that pulled Kay Leonard together. Since she had left the airliner her whole mind had been occupied with Kelley, and with thoughts of Rayburn and Wallis who had died. She shook her head as if to clear her mind. Then she said:

'Hatch, give me a hand to look at the wounded.'

'Sure.' Connors looked around vaguely as if uncertain where to start. Then Kelley gestured at the two unconscious forms on the ground.

'Fix them first,' he said. 'I'm okay for a bit.'

Connors and the girl knelt beside the lean body of the Frenchman and the navigator gently pulled back the man's red-soaked shirt. A bullet had penetrated the right side of the man's chest and as there was no exit hole in his back it was apparently still lodged inside.

Connors said grimly. 'I don't think there's a lot we can do for him.'

Kay Leonard watched a watery trickle of blood bubble out of the unconscious man's chest, and shuddered.

'We've got to try anyway,' she said. She stood up and lifting her blue skirt pulled her slip from underneath it. She stepped out of the white silk and tore it open. With clenched fingers she ripped off a wide strip and bunched it up into a pad. Kneeling by the injured man she dabbed at his bleeding chest and then pressed the pad over the bullet hole.

She handed Connors the rest of the slip. 'Rip it into strips, Hatch, we'll bind him up.' She waited for him to complete the task, then, with Navarr helping Connors to support the man, she bound several strips around his chest, taping the pad firmly into place.

Navarr asked quietly. 'Will he live?'

'I don't know. I don't think so.' Kay wiped the sweat from her eyes and the back of her neck. The movement smeared the red trickle that marred the whiteness of her throat more widely over the soft flesh. There was nothing more they could do for the Frenchman, so she turned her attention to the Chinese.

There was nothing they could do for him, either. The man was dead. A bullet had entered the left-hand side of his back and while they had carried him across he had died.

Kay stood up. 'All right, Scott, let me see that arm.'

Kelley gritted his teeth while she gently took off his uniform jacket and then tore away what was left of the sleeve of his shirt. A bullet had shattered his upper arm, and streams of red were running down below his elbow. It was obvious that the bone was splintered but there was nothing she could do except wipe the worst of the blood away and bind the limb to keep it clean. Gentle though she was, the operation almost caused Kelley to black out again. Sweat drenched his forehead, and Connors had to hold him by the waist to prevent him from falling.

When she had finished the bandaging, the air hostess took off her jacket and slipped her shoulders out of her white blouse. Replacing the jacket over her brassière she made the blouse into a rough sling, tying the sleeves behind Kelley's neck.

Apart from minor cuts and a variety of bruises none of the others was hurt.

By now the blazing airliner had almost

burnt itself out. The first stages of shock were beginning to wear off, and only the bespectacled little Englishwoman still cried. For long moments they stood there regarding each other uncomfortably. Then the American eyed Connors and demanded:

'Well, what happened?'

Navarr said sarcastically: 'There was a cow on the road.'

Connors gave him a warning look that was mostly a request for silence, then he said to the American: 'Didn't you see, sir? We were shot down.'

'No, I didn't see, son. If I had I wouldn't be asking would I? I was asleep when you guys started sky-larking all over the God-damned place.'

Connors glanced around the party and addressed them all.

'I don't know how many of you did see it but that's what happened. A fighter plane simply shot us out of the sky. Where it came from or why it did it I don't know. The plane carried no markings. She came out of the sun, and didn't give the pilot a chance.'

Kelley addded grimly: 'And if we hadn't had a bloody good pilot, who hung on with his guts spilling out, we'd have nose-dived smack into the jungle. Jim Rayburn fought that plane down to the last.'

The American looked slightly abashed, then he said harshly:

'That's not possible. Nobody would dare atack an aeroplane just like that. Nobody would have reason to.'

Kelley said angrily: 'You ought to have been on the other plane! You could have told that to the fighter pilot.'

'Now look, son — '

'And don't bloody well son me, either!' The pain in Kelley's arm was making him sharp tempered.

Connors said evenly. 'You people know as much as we do. It seems unbelievable, I know, but you all felt the impact as that fighter sprayed us with bullets.'

'Goddamn it! My embassy's gonna hear about this!'

'Are you going to post them a letter or catch yourself a carrier pigeon?' Navarr had taken an instinctive dislike to the arrogant-mouthed American and just couldn't resist the sneer.

The American looked angry, but the easy way the tall cynic leaned against the boulders held him in check. Before he could speak Kay Leonard acted as peacemaker.

'Let's not quarrel,' she said quietly. 'We're not in an exactly enviable position here, and it'll do no good to fight among ourselves. The only thing for us to do is to think about how to get out.'

'Well?' demanded the American. 'How *do* we get out?'

No one answered, and finally Kelley said tightly:

'That's a bloody good question. Should be worth sixty thousand dollars in any quiz show.'

Kay squeezed his arm.

'Easy, Scott,' she muttered softly.

The American looked as though he was about to make a come-back answer when suddenly Lorretta said:

'He's coming round.'

A low moan echoed her words and they turned to find her kneeling over the injured Frenchman. The man was moving weakly, and another low moan escaped his lips. They gathered around him slowly and Kay knelt with the blonde actress to help her to support the man's head.

'M'sieur Larrieux,' she recalled his name from the passenger list and spoke it softly. 'M'sieur Larrieux, can you hear me?'

Larrieux's eyelids flickered then opened. He looked up into her face and another spasm of pain racked his frame. The sweat lay like bubbling oil on his temples. He opened his mouth and the thin lips moved without speaking.

'Don't talk,' Kay told him softly. 'You'll be all right.'

'Non, non,' fresh sweat formed. 'I am dying, ma'm'selle, listen — listen closely. It was for me that they shot the aeroplane down. They cannot afford for me to live. You must get back — get back and tell them. Many thousands will die if they succeed. Men, women, children, all will die. One of you must tell what I know. One of you *must* survive . . . '

3

Too Dangerous to Live

Larrieux's faltering words made Kay cease her gentle entreaties for him to remain silent. His death was only a matter of time, and it was obvious that the Frenchman had something important to tell.

Connors said quietly:

'You mean you know why we were shot down?'

Larrieux made a slight motion of his dark head that might have been intended as a nod.

'Oui, the airliner was shot down to ensure that I never reach Hanoi alive. I knew I was too dangerous for Voron to let me live but — ' he choked ' — but I did not think he could go that far.'

'But why?' Connors tone was tense. 'Why couldn't they let you live?'

'That — that is what I must tell you.

Please listen. I will start at the beginning. I — I think I can live long enough to tell my story.'

Kay Leonard lifted the man's head a little and settled it in her lap as she knelt behind him. 'Take it easy, M'sieur. You have plenty of time, just try not to exert yourself. We're listening.'

'Thank you.' Larrieux licked his thin lips and groaned slightly as he tried to move his arm. Kay held the arm still. The Frenchman said weakly. 'First I ought to tell you who I am. My name is Pierre Larrieux, I work for a section of the French Intelligence Service, something similar to the English M.I.5.'

Leo Rex, the American, said angrily: 'Aw can the build up. I wanna know why we were shot down.'

Connors said tightly: 'Shut up Mister before I shut you up. Let him tell it in his own way.'

Rex glowered but remained silent.

Larrieux told his story weakly and without any further interruptions. At times his voice wavered but never really died out. Only when the fierce spasms of pain vibrated through his smashed chest did he stop. Then he tensed, streaming sweat as he fought down the pain. In those moments Kay Leonard smoothed his temples and wiped away the sweat with the small handful of silk that remained from her torn slip.

The others watched and listened in silence. There was nothing that they could do.

Larrieux's story was clear, despite the weakness of his voice and despite the fact that he could only gasp out the main details of what had happened to him. As he struggled to tell his tale, he lived again in his mind the events which had brought him to this pass . . .

He had been sent to Nakai on a special assignment by his office in Paris. Soon after the trouble began to boil over in the islands, a report had reached his superiors informing them that a known communist agent, named Voron, had recently appeared on the island, posing as a legitimate businessman. The Air Force security authorities had been warned, and Larrieux had been loaned to the

American department to help them to discover the man's intentions. Larrieux had the advantage of knowing Voron by sight, and the Americans had been glad to have him.

Voron was a particularly dangerous agent who had worked against the French in Indo China, and it was there that Larrieux had got a glimpse of him. At the time Voron had been drinking in a bar, and had not known that the man observing him from a darkened corner was an agent of the French Intelligence Service. Voron's presence in Nakai was clear evidence that something big was brewing, something that meant trouble for the Americans. Voron was no small-time soap-box-orator and riot-rouser. He was one of the most skilful agents that the communists possessed. If Voron was in Nakai then he was most certainly not there to incite rioting, which his less dangerous comrades were managing quite well on their own. And he wasn't there for pleasure either. That meant that it was imperative that Larrieux found out what he was there for — and found it out in time to kill the scheme before it had a chance to develop. He had recognised the communist agent two days after he flew into Nakai, and from then on Voron had been watched day and night by a team of specially picked American security agents. The communist had taken a cheap room in one of the small, recently built hotels in the fast growing capital town, and to all outward appearances he was engaged in some normal press work. Despite constant survey he did nothing and contacted no one that might give them a lead. For over a week the round-the-clock guard on his movements was kept up. Then Voron gave the American team the slip.

It was simply done. There was a man posted both at the back and the front of the hotel to keep watch, and within easy reach of each was a nondescript car complete with a driver and a powerful engine. If Voron left the hotel the foot guard followed him at a discreet distance with the car crawling through the crowded streets well behind. If Voron boarded a taxi or a bus, the car was signalled up to take over. Afterwards it became painfully obvious that Voron had become aware of these arrangements. It was eight o'clock in the morning when he walked calmly down the front steps of his hotel. Then without warning a fast car raced up the road, slackened slightly, and the enemy agent made a suicide leap on the running board. The car accelerated and shot away.

Pierre Larrieux had been watching the front of the hotel that morning, hidden by a bamboo screen that fenced off a disused yard. He saw Voron take his wild jump on to the speeding car and realised that they had lost him. Then luck broke in his direction. The spluttering roar of an engine heralded a smoke-streaming motor-cycle that any museum would have been glad to own. It was being ridden in bottom gear by a wide-eyed native boy of about eleven who was clinging terrified to the saddle. Where he had stolen it from Larrieux didn't stop to think. He ran out and scooped the little brown body out of the saddle. Dropping him roughly he ran alongside the bike, keeping it upright with one hand. In another second he had jumped astride, grated through the gears, and was flat out after Voron's disappearing car.

Behind him the little wide-eyed boy stared after him in bewilderment. Then he began to cry, whether at relief from escaping from the monster of smoke and noise, or at the thought of what he was going to tell older companions who had seated him upon the machine he wasn't sure. He only knew that he had reason to cry. He stood in the middle of the dusty road with the tears running down his fat face. His ragged and dirty trousers subsided slowly down to his ankles because the string about his waist had come undone, but he didn't care. Then a tall white man in the uniform of the U.S.A.F. came towards him with a sheepish grin. The boy's crying wavered hesitantly as the tall man knelt in the dusty road in front of him. The American gave him two packets of chewing gum, three nickels, and instructions to pull his goddamn pants up. The boy began to smile again. The motor-cyle was forgotten.

In the saddle of the ancient, smoke-pouring machine Larrieux was desperately trying to keep his quarry in sight as it twisted through the battered taxies, bullock carts, bicycles and swarming pedestrians, that filled the maze of narrow streets. He drew angry batteries of curses in a torrent of different dialects as he smothered the unfortunates he passed in oily black smoke clouds. The machine was bouncing like a solid steel bronco beneath him, and he realised painfully that it had been made long before springs were invented. He was more than glad when Voron's car had to slow down to wind through the swarming masses that cluttered the native market, it meant that he could slow down too.

There was no road here, just dusty, hard-packed earth trampled down by the constant passage of thousands of shuffling feet, as the shouting and jostling crowds harried the smiling fruit and poultry sellers who squatted among their wares. The din was tremendous, a yelling, screaming cacophony of sound, punctuated by the cackle of doomed chickens and the yelping barks of the lean and scruffy dogs. The big black car that had whisked Voron away nosed through it with its horn blaring wildly. Larieux kept fifty yards behind the car, confident that here at least they could not see him following, and tried vainly to get some kind of note out of the perished bulb horn that was tied on to the handlebars of his machine. Finally the whisp of dirty string that secured the horn fell apart and he left the implement behind in the road.

He came out of the market area in time to see Voron's car streaking away up a rutted street, flanked with rough wooden shacks with corrugated iron roofs. He raced after it, wrenching and twisting at the handlebars as he fought to keep the wheels of his cycle out of the deep cart-ruts that would have thrown him off. He was on the poorer outskirts of the town now, heading away from the fast growing modern buildings.

The streets were almost empty here and he let the big black car get well ahead. The car had slowed speed in order to manoeuvre the rough roads, and Larrieux knew that here he was most likely to be spotted. Then a creaking, rickety bus suddenly lurched out of a crossroads ahead and he had to brake violently. The bike slewed round and Larrieux had to hop round in a half-circle as he strained to hold up the angled machine beneath him.

The bus churned away and Larrieux swore in a stream of purple French. The dust cloud he had stirred up cut his curses short and turned them into a fit of choking. He straightened the bike and started it up again. In the dust cloud kicked up by the bus he could see nothing and bitter rage swelled within him.

He drove right into the dust cloud and then steered to one side so that he could see past the lumbering vehicle. Solemn brown faces watched him from the back of the bus, jammed up against the glass of the window like so many baked beans in a tin, only with features and scrubby carpets of black hair. A chicken squawked at him noisily and he swore at it in French. On the roof of the bus was a mound of carelessly tied baskets and bundles, and he realised abruptly that riding too close beneath that load could be a hazardous business. He was almost blind now from the swirling dust clouds and his eyes smarted like fury as he looked for Voron's car. Then he saw it, still nosing along a hundred yards or so in front of the bus, and maintaining the same steady speed.

He realised that the bus could prove a lucky break for him. If Voron's vehicle didn't increase speed, and provided he could stick the dust, he could remain hidden behind the bus. For several minutes he held the motor-cycle in that position, keeping well up and a little to one side of the swaying bus in order to avoid the thickest of the dust cloud. Then he realised that this position was directly below the jerking mound of luggage on the bus roof. He tightened his lips against the probing dust and hoped that the ropes would hold.

The road led out of Nakai and climbed up steeply towards a low saddle-back ridge that would bring them down into a smaller town on the other side of the island. The surface was merely a rough track which had been levelled since the Americans took over, and on either side there was a wall of low scrub which gave way to tangled jungle. Several times they passed through feathery curtains of bamboo, and as they neared the top of the low pass they had to wind round outcrops of boulders which were almost hidden in a tangle of vines and vegetation.

They began the descent towards the sea, and through slitted eyes Larrieux saw the straw and wooden shacks of the old town below them. Over to the left he could see the single runway of the civilian airport that had been built before Nakai began to grow. The descent was through low scrub and grassland and once they passed a group of natives lying under the shade of a sprawling Banyan tree. They were lean, beaming little men, wearing gay-coloured loin cloths that wound around their legs to their knees. Their skins were a dark glistening brown and they waved and cat-called at the occupants of the bus. The yelling passengers gave as good as they got, and burst into a torrent of laughter as the loungers were swallowed in the dust cloud.

Larrieux stuck close to the bus all the way into the town, ignoring the curious comments from those inside. He was nearly blind now from the pain of his smarting eyes, but he knew that he couldn't possibly have to hold out much longer. This road only led to the town and then on to the airport, and there was only another mile or two to go. He was aching all over from the constant jarring of the springless bike and his arms felt as though they were being wrenched out of their sockets. He was more than relieved when the big black car carrying Voron finally turned off the road before entering the pitiful tumble of dwellings that made up the only other town on the main island.

The moment he saw Voron turn off, Larrieux slackened speed and ran his borrowed motor-cycle off the road. The bus vanished into the town in a swirling cloud of dust, and the squawking chicken in the back cackled a shrill good-bye. Larrieux ran his bike down a slight incline into a tangle of ferns where it would be out of sight, and then hurried along in the shadows of the massed palms that overhung the road.

He had made himself familiar with the layout of the island within hours of landing and he knew full well that there was no road where Voron could have taken the car. He must have stopped it just off the road and be continuing on foot, in which case he might have seen the motor-cycle go past. That was why Larrieux had quitted the machine straight away. If Voron had noticed the cycle before they had left Nakai he might have guessed the truth, and Larrieux was too cautious to take chances.

When he reached the spot where Voron had turned off, the Frenchman saw the big black car standing empty, fifty yards up a narrow track that dwindled into a mere footpath that vanished up a wooded hillside. On his left were the massed palms and on the right of the track a flat expanse of low grass, dotted with boulders, bamboo clumps, and light copses of bush and shrub that sloped down to the village. Larrieux searched for any sign of movement, but of the men he was following there was nothing to be seen. He decided swiftly that they must have followed the narrow path up the hillside and he ran lightly past the stationary car.

He started up the hillside and ducked into cover in the shade of thick branches, hidden for a few moments by the leafy curtain of green. Here he stopped and drew an automatic pistol out of his pocket, he checked that the ammunition clip was in place and that the gun was ready to fire. Then he spat on the palm of his right hand before closing it around the cold butt. He was just about to start up the hillside when the sound of a car engine stopped him.

He froze silently, all his senses alert and his muscles quivering slightly with the tension. He saw a battered Ford saloon come up the road from the village, churning up a dust screen that made it almost unrecognisable. The car stopped on the road exactly opposite Voron's black car and then reversed into the track behind it. The driver switched off the ignition, and two men climbed out. Both were Orientals, but whereas one wore the clothes and features of a semi-prosperous Chinese, the second man was obviously in the worker class. He wore the ragged remains of a woollen jersey and a pair of filthy grey trousers, and his features marked him as a Burmese.

The Chinese walked up to Voron's car and gave a toothy grin that dwarfed the rest of his face. He turned and said something to the ragged one who nodded without expression. They passed the car and approached the hillside where Larrieux waited.

The Frenchman knew instinctively that they were here to meet Voron. Slowly and cautiously he backed into the tangled barrier of vegetation which flanked the path beneath the cooling trees. The oncoming pair were close and he dared not back too far into the undergrowth in case they heard the rustle of his movements. He wetted his lips and sank to his knees, making himself as inconspicuous as possible, the automatic ready in his hand.

The two men passed within a yard of him, so close that he caught the unwashed smell of the ragged one and the sickly scent of the Chinese. Both were talking in a dialect he did not understand, and the wide-mouthed Chinaman was still beaming his toothy grin. The ragged one, who was dark-skinned with sleek, pitch black hair, didn't look quite so comfortable. His bare, dirt-encrusted feet were dragging slightly as he walked.

Larrieux let them get well ahead before he straightened up and followed them as silently as possible. The path led almost straight up the hillside, but in most places it was so overgrown that he had to force his way through. The jungle had a damp, clinging smell about it and the heat began to make him sweat. He caught the sweet scent of Jasmine from a colourful array of bushes in a spot where the sun struck through the thinning trees, and several times he was whipped by the springy green branches. The vegetation thinned out suddenly and he heard voices ahead. Cautiously he dropped on his stomach, and began to worm his way along the path. The undergrowth almost closed above his head, and he had a sudden horror of coming face to face with a snake. He shivered as he crawled along.

The path ended suddenly and he lay motionless on the fringe of a small clearing. Ahead there was a raised hut with a small veranda and a palm-thatched roof. Voron, thin-nosed and sharp-eyed, was leaning on the veranda rail of thick bamboo. Beside him stood a dark-skinned man of Asian origin whom Larrieux knew must be the driver of Voron's car. They were greeting the two men whom Larrieux had just followed up the hillside. Above them the sun was a glaring white mass in an almost colourless sky. Behind them was a ring of jungle green; a barrier of leafy branches and dark twisting vines, choked by the ever present mass of vegetation and brightened by the reds and golds of orchids and the pink flowers of tall frangipani trees. A flock of coloured parrots erupted from the background and made Larrieux start with alarm.

The wide-mouthed Chinaman answered Voron with a stream of dialect, and the communist agent scowled. 'Speak in English, Kang, it is a language the three of us can understand.'

Kang looked sulky. He gestured to his ragged companion and said sullenly: 'He does not speak English.'

Voron glanced at the man. 'He only has to do as he's told, perhaps it is as well that he does not understand everything.' He favoured the man with a hard look and the Burmese scuffed his bare foot uncomfortably in the grass. Voron went on: 'Come inside, all of you.'

The three men followed him up on to the veranda and into the hut while Larrieux cursed silently. Through an open window in the bamboo wall he saw the Chinese Kang, but the others were out of sight, and he couldn't hear what they were saying. He felt the sweat run down his back and split into twin streams either side of his waist as he lay there straining his ears, but they had all lowered their voices. Whatever they were discussing was something they didn't want overheard.

Larrieux weighed up the risks and realised that somehow he had to get under the raised floor of that hut. Now that a lucky break had brought him almost within hearing he couldn't just lie there and throw the chance away. If he simply waited for them to finish and followed Voron back again to his hotel he would be back exactly where he had started. He would just have to take the risk of crossing that open space.

There didn't appear to be any of the four keeping a lookout and that and the reassuring weight of the automatic in his hand gave Larrieux the courage to make the gamble. If he were seen he would just have to shoot his way out of it and nothing would be lost. He could easily give them the slip in the jungle. He rose slowly to his knees and then, pistol held at the ready, he sprinted swiftly across those few yards of open space.

His feet made no sound on the soft grass and in a matter of seconds he was crouching against the bamboo wall of the hut; his heart was racing frantically and his mouth was dry. Sweat was drenching his shirt and he was trembling a little. Only the automatic was rock-steady in his hand.

The expected outcry of alarm from inside never came and with an effort to steady his heart-beats he realised that he had got away with it. He could hear the voices more clearly now, and he crawled underneath the raised hut until he was directly below them. He lay there, sweating and straining his ears to catch all that they were saying.

'He knows what he has to do,' Kang was saying, his voice vaguely hesitant as he used his uncertain English. 'I have told him many many times.'

Voron said harshly: 'Tell him many many more times. Apart from this fool there is nothing that can go wrong. You must make certain that he does exactly what he is told. You will be held responsible.'

'He will succeed,' Kang assured him. 'It is a simple job to smuggle the case into the air base, and all he has to do then is to hide it aboard one of the planes.'

'Yes, but we also want the identification number of the plane he chooses. How can we know when the plane with our parcel is taking off if we do not know that?'

'He will do it,' Kang insisted. 'I have told him so many times. He will hide the parcel where it will not be found and then write the registration number of the aircraft on a piece of paper. I have spent hours teaching him to write figures and letters. He will be able to copy the number.'

'All right,' Voron sounded satisfied. 'But when it is done you will inform Calostro. He will be in charge from now on. Somehow the Americans have become aware of my presence and I am watched. It is too dangerous for me to contact you anymore. Calostro will be in complete command, and you will assist him in every possible way. The moment the package is aboard one of the American planes you will contact him and report. Then, together, you will keep a day and night watch over the radio, it is already turned in to the frequency used by the air base control tower. You will keep a check on all the normal clearance calls between the tower controller and the pilots of the aeroplanes. The moment you hear our plane identify itself and ask for clearance for take-off, one of you will leave the radio and watch the plane leave the ground through field-glasses. The instant that the plane is airborne you will signal the man at the radio to activate the nuclear war-head in the package by remote control. It will blast the air base off the map.'

Calostro, who had to be the driver of the black car, said calmly: 'Are you sure the explosion will be big enough? The parcel is no larger than a small suitcase.'

'It will be big enough. Not a full powered nuclear blast of course, but big enough to destroy the air base completely.' The communist laughed suddenly. 'And the joy of it all is that the Americans themselves will be blamed. Everybody knows that no rocket missile or enemy bomber could hit the base without being detected by radar and reported before actual impact. The fact that there was no report will bear out what the few who survive will be able to say, namely that one of the cursed American's own bombers exploded in the air.'

Calostro laughed with him. 'It is the perfect plan all right! We rid ourselves of an enemy air base and strike a great blow against American prestige at the same time. The fools will be branded as careless idiots who relaxed safety precautions, and it is unlikely that any other neutral government will allow them to build bases on their soil. And we shall not even be suspected.'

Kang said enthusiastically: 'And with the Great Soviet all ready to rush supplies and medicines to the stricken islanders the whole of Asia will be able to see who their real friends are.'

Voron chuckled.

'That is so. But now, are there any questions? You all know exactly what to do? Calostro knows where the radio and the equipment for firing the bomb by remote control are hidden.

The hideout is on the mountainside, but well screened by a ridge of rock so you will be quite safe. A third man is ready to help you when the time comes, so you have no excuse for not keeping a constant watch. Remember that the plane must be airborne before you blow it up. For one thing the effects of the blast will have a wider range of destruction from about fifty feet above ground level, and for another it will be seen by a lot more people who will be able to report. The few that live, that is.'

Calostro answered evenly: 'We both understand, everything will take place as you have directed.'

'That is good, because everything is now in your hands. I must return to my hotel and allow myself to be watched by the police. A getaway like this last one will not work a second time. Now for the last time, is there anything you are unsure about?'

'Nothing,' said Calostro.

'I too, have nothing,' Kang added.

'All right.' Voron sounded very confident and pleased with himself. 'Now we will split up and get away from here. There is nothing more we can do until this poor fool has planted our little surprise package. Afterwards, of course, he must be eliminated.'

Kang said flatly: 'I will kill him.'

'Good! Now let us get back.'

Larrieux heard them start moving above him. Cautiously he wriggled towards the rear of the hut, praying that they would leave straight away and not hang around. If he were spotted underneath the hut it would spell his death, for after what he had heard Voron would waste no mercy upon him. And trapped beneath the hut he wouldn't stand a chance of getting out alive.

That last thought made him realise that the risk of discovery would be no greater if he was standing up behind the hut where he would be out of sight. And if things should go wrong he would stand a much better chance of shooting his way out by being already on his feet. Swiftly he wriggled from underneath the hut, scraping the back of his neck as he snaked backwards. By half-kneeling down he could still see the other side, and he saw the legs of Voron and his companions as they stepped off the veranda. Cautiously he inched nearer to the edge of the hut so that he could see the path into the jungle and watch them go.

It was then that Voron let out an angry exclamation in Russian.

Larrieux saw the reason in exactly the same instant: right in the centre of the open space that Voron had to cross there lay a large white handkerchief. Larrieux recognised it as his own and swore silently as he realised that he must have dropped it. In the same moment he knew that it would take no more than split seconds for Voron to discover that none of his own party had dropped the handkerchief.

Larrieux knew that only a surprise dash could save him now. He launched himself from his knees like a sprinter, out into the open and straight at the footpath. As he cleared the shelter of the hut he fired twice underneath his left arm and saw the four men frantically scatter. The sharp reports of the automatic shocked the still morning air, and then he was crashing into the jungle and along the path. He stretched his arm behind him and fired blindly as he vanished from the clearing, knowing that he couldn't score a hit, but hoping to keep them at bay.

Branches, vines, and ferns, whipped and clutched at his hurtling body as he raced down the jungle-shrouded hillside. He thought of the battered Ford that faced the road and prayed that the key was still in the ignition. If he could reach it he could hold them off with the gun while he started the engine and be away before they could turn the second car in pursuit.

He could hear them crashing as they came after him, blundering heavily along the path. Startled birds flew screeching into the air as he passed and above their cries rose the bark of a second automatic. Then a third. Two different guns were streaming bullets down the hillside in a blind quest to stop his fleeing form. He saw leaves fly and branches splinter to his left, and then suddenly he broke out of cover before the big black car.

He saw the Ford beyond it and sprinted up the now level track. Then, as he drew level with the black car, he saw a man standing behind the open door of the Ford. He cursed bitterly as he realised that Kang had left a guard behind him. The man must have been sitting inside the car when they left and Larrieux, with his mind on the other two, had not noticed him. The man was raising a gun when Larrieux took a snap shot at him and made him duck back into the Ford. The bullet hit the car door with a resounding clang and ricocheted off into the palms.

Larrieux looked round wildly as he heard Voron and the others slithering down through the jungle behind him. Then he wrenched open the door of the black car. He swung in behind the wheel and found the key in the ignition. He jerked the starter and nothing happened. Savagely he switched the key over and then Voron and Kang came out of the jungle together. Larrieux thrust his arm through the open window of the car and fired twice to send them scurrying back into cover. Again he tried the starter with his other hand and the engine sparked noisily. Shots from the man in the Ford banged tinnily into the black car as he started it up and ramming it into gear he stamped on the pedal. Steering with one hand he fired twice as the car lunged to where Voron and his companions were again scattering.

At the last moment, the Frenchman spun the wheel and swerved the car away. He dropped his automatic into his pocket and had to use both hands to control the car as she bounced over the rough ground to the right of the track. She ploughed through a clump of bushes and ferns and he fought her around to face the road. He had to wrench at the wheel to avoid a boulder as he aimed the car at an angle that would take him clear of the man in the Ford who was still shooting erratically. The jolting made his teeth rattle, and almost threw him through the roof as the black car surged forward crazily in low gear. A patch of young bamboo splintered and crushed beneath the rolling tyres, and then a small hillock made one side of the car rear up and then down again like a ship in the fury of a storm. Larrieux hung on until she hit the dirt road and he realised that he was still cut off.

The man in the Ford had driven it square across the road, and there was no way of getting round it. His route to Nakai was blocked.

Angrily Larrieux spun the wheel and followed the dusty road in the other direction into the village, accelerating as he went. A quick glance over his shoulder showed Voron and the other three racing towards the Ford. He wiped the streaming sweat from his eyes and settled down to drive, sending the car lurching and bouncing between the rough shacks of the village.

There was only one place that Larrieux could go to now, and that was the end of the road, to the civilian airport that lay beyond the village. There he could find a telephone and report. That was his sole thought now, to get a report through to the American Security Forces before Voron caught up with him. That report *had* to go through.

He glanced back once and saw the

Ford rattling along behind him, then he put his foot down and raced all out for the airport. He roared out of the village and up a narrow but level road that was flanked with swaying bamboo groves that recoiled with fluttering fronds in the wind of his passing. He glanced back again, and saw that the Ford had dropped well behind, but when he looked back a few seconds later he saw that it was picking up again and that now there were only four men in it instead of five. The Burmese had been dropped off but he had no time to wonder why.

The passenger buildings of the airport loomed ahead some minutes later and Larrieux braked violently before them. He was out of the car and running up the paved approach to the main entrance within seconds. He spotted a public telephone just inside the hall and dived into it. Swiftly he dialled his number and then slipped his hand back into his pocket and around his automatic while he waited. His eyes watched the hall entrance.

He saw Voron, Kang and Calostro

enter the hall together and in the same moment realised why the Burmese had been dropped off. The telephone line had been cut.

He replaced the receiver as the three men separated and saw them move to different vantage points about the hall. The right hand of each one, like Larrieux's own, was firmly entrenched in his jacket pocket. The airport staff still hurried about their business, to them nothing was amiss.

Larrieux stepped slowly out of the telephone booth. Voron moved to meet him. The Frenchman was sweating but his nerves were steady.

Voron said flatly: 'It is fortunate that I anticipated your first move. You are dangerous, my friend.'

Larrieux's face showed no expression. He said: 'I'm taking you with me Voron. It doesn't matter which one of your men guns me down. My shot is for you.'

'Don't be crude, my friend. Shooting is the last thing I want. If I gunned you down, as you put it, there would be a hue and cry that would turn this island upside down. That sort of thing is all right out in the hills, but not in a public airport. The repercussions would ruin my plans. Of course, if you force my hand by attempting to pass on a message then it will not matter anyway. Until then it is stalemate.'

Larrieux smiled. 'I see. You dare not start a gun battle here in front of witnesses, for apart from knowing that one of you at least will die with me, it will mean the collapse of your plans. While I dare not act without inviting certain death! A pretty situation, but it can't last.'

'No, but it gives us a time lapse in which to think.'

Larrieux drew a breath. 'All right, so I've thought.' He moved towards the booking counter, still watching Voron.

Larrieux knew that to leave the airport the way he had arrived meant death. Voron and his accomplices would follow and kill him the moment he left the crowds. Also, the present situation couldn't last. One of them had to make a move. He preferred to take the initiative himself. Calmly he asked the Indian girl behind the counter which was the next plane to leave. The answer was Flight Eighteen for Hanoi, due to leave in thirty-three minutes. Larrieux booked a seat, the only way out, and then smiled at Voron.

'Your move.'

Voron laughed.

'Admirable. You play a war of nerves and hope for time. Enough action to put me in a quandary, but not enough to spark off our gun battle. Very well.' He nodded Calostro over and said evenly. 'Book a seat on Flight Eighteen for our friend who is on his way. Meet the car outside and hand him the ticket. He will know what to do.'

Calostro grinned and moved off to obey. He gave Larrieux no chance to hear the name in which the passage was booked.

Voron was smiling. 'This is working out well. Kang and I will watch you until take-off, then our unknown friend will take over. Any attempt to pass on a message, and you will die, for if you succeed, an upheaval on this island would not matter any more. You may get a chance to talk before my agent gets an opportunity to kill you without fuss — but I doubt it. My agent is an expert.'

Larrieux didn't answer. Still watching both Kang and Voron he moved into the lounge and positioned himself with his back to a corner of the bar. It was still stalemate.

The long half-hour until the airliner finally took off was an ordeal he hoped never to face again. It seemed impossible that he could actually be standing there with his hand coiled about the gun in his pocket, not daring to move or even speak to anyone in case he should start off a blaze of gunfire. Impossible, also, that in this crowd of people two communist agents could he watching him like hawks, also with automatics gripped in their hands and concealed in their jacket pockets. He could feel the clammy presence of death all around him.

He watched his fellow passengers arrive, and the entry of each one screwed his nerves tighter. Any of them could be Voron's agent. There was just no way of knowing. As the lounge filled, the tension built up to screaming point.

He felt a vast feeling of relief when he was finally able to quit the airport, even though he knew that Voron's unknown agent must now be in the crowd around him. He knew that as long as he remained silent he was safe in the crowds. For that reason he made no attempt to contact the pilot and use the plane's radio while they were in flight. He had already decided that his chance would come when they reached Hanoi. The unknown agent could not stick too close without giving himself away, and Larrieux only had to be first through any door in the airport buildings and he could slam it on the rest of the passengers and be away. He only needed a split second start.

Four hours later he realised how neatly Voron had tricked him. Voron's smooth story of a mystery agent watching his every move had caused him to keep his mouth shut, but Voron had had no need to plant a man on the plane to kill him. The airliner cruised slowly compared to the top speeds of up to a thousand five hundred m.p.h. reached by modern interceptor-fighters. And in the hours that it had been in the air there had been plenty of time for Voron to radio for a high-speed machine to blast the airliner out of the sky, eliminating Larrieux and every possible witness without trace.

The stakes were high. And Voron was a very thorough worker.

4

The Grim Truth

There was a long silence when the Frenchman had finished his story, such of it as his condition permitted him to tell. He lay with his head still resting on Kay Leonard's lap, breathing weakly, his face glistening and creased with pain. The others looked down at him without speaking; doubting the credibility of his story. Farther up the green river of the valley the broken wreckage of the airliner was burning itself out, hidden from view by sluggish smoke clouds that hung low over the scene through the lack of wind to disperse them. Overhead the glaring sun still radiated its strength-sapping, sweat-drawing heat. Around them the jungle maze of branch and vine, dark twisted boles, and sun-mottled greenery, rustled vaguely with hidden life. The silence lengthened until Larrieux's harsh breathing seemed to swell out of all proportion, rasping ominously in his throat as though every draught of air was liable to break into a death rattle and choke him. The silk strips that bound up his painfully heaving chest were already stained with his slowly seeping blood.

Steve Navarr eyed his companions thoughtfully as they considered the Frenchman's words. Kelley's pain-tightened face was worried, his temples creased beneath his fair hair. Connors looked grim. The Greek was undecided. The actress looked as though she didn't know what to think, while the arrogant-mouthed American was obviously sceptical. The faces of the two Chinese were inscrutable; there was just no expression on them at all. Schelde looked unhappy, his rounded face almost mournful. The bespectacled Englishwoman was still too grief-stricken to care, while the face of the air hostess showed only concern for the dying man before her.

At last Kelley said slowly: 'Are you quite sure about this, M'sieur? It seems pretty long lengths to go to, just to kill one man.'

Larrieux had to stiffen himself to fight off another surge of pain before he could answer. 'I am sure.' His voice was weak and forced. 'When you consider the stakes it becomes the most logical thing to do. Voron knew that if he or one of his men were to start shooting at the airport and murdered me in front of witnesses, then the whole island would be turned upside down in the hunt for my killers. His secret radio installation might have been discovered. Some of his men might have been roped in during the search and broken down under questioning. He himself would have had to flee the island for he was already known to the American Security Department. There were a dozen ways in which he could have ruined the chances of his scheme being a success. But in this way, by shooting down the airliner, he not only kills me but all the witnesses to my death as well. Nobody survives to tell the tale, and there are no repercussions on the island. Voron can go on with his plans exactly as arranged.'

The effort of talking had sapped more of Larrieux's fading strength and he closed his eyes as he fought for breath. Kay Leonard wiped the streaming sweat from his greying face, watching him with worried eyes.

Hatch Connors said grimly: 'Well, there has to be an explanation, and the very fact that we were shot down seems to prove his story.' He was looking at Kelley as he spoke.

Before Kelley could answer the American cut in insolently:

'I figure it's a load of crap! This Voron guy just wouldn't dare try anything like that. Besides he hasn't a dawg's chance of getting away with it. Nobody could smuggle a nuclear bomb aboard one of Uncle Sam's planes. It just ain't possible.'

Kelley said tightly: 'It could be done. The air police can't possibly search every truck and van that enters the base. The bomb could be smuggled through. And a native workman, who probably moves like a cat in the dark, would be just the man to hide it aboard an unguarded plane. The thing is possible all right, and if anything goes wrong this Voron and his crew are undoubtedly ready to bolt and leave the native holding the baby.'

'I still just don't believe it, son.'

The word 'son' rankled Kelley again and Connors had to cut in swiftly.

'In that case, mister, just you suggest a better explanation. That man on the ground is dying, and if you think that he's made up a fancy yarn on the spur of the moment just for the hell of it you must be crazy. A man who's dying in agony only forces himself to talk when he's got something to say.'

Navarr, who had been listening thoughtfully, decided that the young airman was right. With that bullet lodged in his chest and his life draining away, Larrieux wouldn't have wasted his last moments in inventing tall stories. Larrieux had to be telling the truth. He looked down at the Frenchman and saw that he obviously hadn't long to live. Fishing in his inside pocket he found a notebook and a ball-point pen, he took them out and knelt by the dying man's side.

'Larrieux,' he spoke the man's name softly. 'Larrieux, can you talk a little more?'

'Oui, I can talk.'

'Then give me a brief description of these men, and anything else we can pass on to your American friends when we get back.'

'You mean if we get back,' the American sneered.

Navarr's mouth hardened and he looked up slowly.

Connors scented trouble, there was something vaguely ominous in the slow movements of the tall cynic. Quickly he stepped between them and faced the American.

'We'll think about that later, Mr. Rex. Right now we've got to find out all that Larrieux can tell us.'

There was a short silence, and then Rex turned away. He sat down sullenly on a boulder and glared at the still smoking remains of their plane farther up the valley.

Navarr said again: 'Try and give me those descriptions Larrieux.'

The Frenchman coughed, then got out weakly: 'Voron needs no description, he is already known. But Calostro is not known: he is about forty to forty-five years old, dark-skinned, medium-built, about five foot ten inches tall. His hair is black and his eyes dark. His features are almost Asian but his jaw is square. Probably he is a Eurasian. The man Kang is a Chinese. He has a very wide mouth, and shows plenty of teeth. He is thin, and about five seven tall. His eyes look almost yellow. The third man, the native, looks like all the other natives. Again he is about five seven tall but he is thickly built. His nose is flat and his hair is sleek and black.' Larrieux paused, fighting for breath again as Navarr's pen raced across his pad in fast shorthand. Then he went on: 'That is the best I can give you. Get my report to Major Roman, he was working with me, he will know what to do.'

Navarr added some notes to the page, and then pocketed the book. 'Okay

Larrieux, we'll get your report to the Major. Just take it easy.' He stood up and wondered how he was going to carry out such a rash promise.

He was still wondering when Kay Leonard said softly: 'I think he's dead.'

They had been expecting that, yet somehow it seemed to hit them out of the blue. One moment the dark Frenchman had been talking weakly, and the next he had simply relaxed and died. There were no last minute dramatics, no choking pleas, or staring eyes. Larrieux had simply told his story and then thankfully relaxed his grip on life. Navarr suddenly realised what an effort it must have cost for the dying man to keep his mind clear and his voice steady in those last moments. Mentally he found a new respect for Pierre Larrieux.

Larrieux's features had found a new peace in death, and Kay Leonard found she couldn't even feel sorry for him as she gently lowered the dark head to the ground. Instead she felt faintly glad that death had at least wiped away the pain and the worry. She stood up slowly and smoothed her skirt, there was a damp, sweat-stained patch in the centre where Larrieux's head had rested but she hardly noticed. She didn't realise that her eyes were wet.

Scott Kelley slipped his good arm around her shoulders and said quietly: 'He had guts. God rest his soul.'

'Amen,' Connors finished.

Navarr echoed him mentally as he looked down at the dead man. Then he glanced slowly around the faces of the others, knowing what they were thinking. They were lost somewhere in the wild jungle-tangled hills of Burma, and on their chances of survival hung the fate of thousands of human beings on the islands of Nakai, the thousands of American servicemen and their families, who, with the native population, would be incinerated if Voron succeeded in the destruction of the mighty air base. And the grim truth was that their own chances of survival without food or water were pitifully slim.

No one voiced his doubt. They stood around in silence, their faces troubled masks that barely hid their thoughts. Navarr glanced at the beautiful Lorretta de Valoise and saw an unexpected firmness in her expression. It surprised him, he wasn't quite sure what he had expected from the temperamental 'Lorretta darling', but he certainly hadn't expected her to remain calm and quiet.

Then Scott Kelley said: 'All right, we'd better give these two a decent burial.' He stood with his feet splayed apart, strands of his fair hair plastered over his damp temples. Blood was showing through his makeshift sling and his boyish face looked grim. Despite his shattered arm he was conscious of the fact that he was still co-pilot, and now that Rayburn was dead he was in charge. He went on:

'There's a low crevice in the rocks over there that will just about take both bodies. Lay them in there and then pile rocks on top. That's the best we can do for them, we've got nothing we can use to dig a proper grave.'

'Why bother?' Rex put the question flatly. 'Why not just sling them in the jungle outa sight?'

Kelley glared at him angrily. 'We'll bury them.' The way he said it made it an order.

Connors said quietly: 'We'd best search them first, Scott. Larrieux should have an automatic on him from the way he talked. We might be able to use that.'

Kelley nodded in agreement and watched as the navigator went through the pockets of the dead Frenchman's clothing. In the jacket pocket he found a small automatic and a spare clip holding ten rounds. There were four shots left in the gun. Another pocket yielded a cigarette lighter and a pack of cigarettes, plus a shiny flick-bladed knife made of Sheffield steel. In an inside pocket was a wallet containing money and identification papers.

Connors held up a celluloid identification wallet. 'I guess this confirms his story, Scott. He definitely was an agent for the French Intelligence Service, and it's unlikely that he would have made up such a yarn.'

'It still sounds crazy,' Rex said.

The co-pilot ignored him and took the

papers from Connors's hand. He nodded in agreement. 'Sure, Hatch, this just about clinches it, there's no doubt that everything he said was true. Somehow we've got to get out of here and pass his report on.' His face went hard. 'When you think of all those people back on Nakai — '

He didn't finish, and no one pressed him to do so.

Connors handed over the gun and the knife, and Kelley thrust them into his pocket while the navigator went through the clothing of the Chinese who had died as they carried him away from the plane. He found another lighter and more cigarettes, but nothing else that would be of any use.

When Connors had finished, they carried the two bodies over to the crevice that Kelley had indicated among the rocks. Carefully they piled up all the loose boulders they could find until the corpses were completely hidden and then Kelley spoke the few words that he could remember of the burial service. They stood in silence for a few moments after

99

that, and then turned wearily away.

Rex loosened his flashy tie and smoothed back his receding hair line. He was a heavy built man but there was a minimum of fat on his large limbs. 'Well?' he demanded. 'What now?'

Kelley answered him. 'First we'll move along the fringe of the jungle, away from those bodies, and there we'll set up a camp of some kind. We'll stay there overnight, and then tomorrow morning, when the plane has cooled, we'll see what we can salvage. After that we'll have to decide whether to stay here and hope that someone will find us, or to rely on our own efforts and attempt to walk out.'

'And what do we do for grub, son? We can't live without food and water.'

Kelley kept his anger in check. 'We'll have to hunt for both,' he said tightly. 'While some of us clear a space to spend the night the others will move into the jungle and try to find some fruit. There's green vegetation all round, watch the birds and see what they eat.'

One of the two Chinese, a shortish man of indefinite age, said cautiously: 'I have been in jungle before, sir. Possibly I can help. I once worked many months in jungles of Viet Nam. I know some fruits that can be eaten.'

'Thank you, Mr. Chang Lee.' Kay Leonard knew all their names from the passenger list and gave him a warm smile.

Chang Lee showed a mouthful of gold teeth somewhat self-consciously, and something that might have been an indication of pleasure crossed his bland face.

Little Wilhem Schelde said suddenly: 'You think it is possible, Captain, that we can find food and water, enough to keep us going until help comes?'

It took Kelley a couple of minutes to realise that the Belgian was addressing him. Then he answered: 'It's possible to live in the jungle, if you know how. We can only hope that between us we possess enough knowledge to stay alive. There must be streams running through hilly country like this, and if we're lucky we might find one. The jungle is full of bird life and provided we go about it the

101

right way we should be able to snare or shoot some. Then, as I said before, there must be edible fruit and berries around us, so theoretically it's quite possible for us to remain alive until we're found.'

Nico Dorapho said quietly: 'It may be possible, Captain, but we must face facts and realise that it is not very probable. There are ten of us to feed and only one little automatic with which to shoot food. There were not more than twelve bullets for that gun and even if you make every shot count, which is impossible, for a tiny pistol is no hunting weapon, they will still last no more than a day or two.'

Kelley knew the dark-skinned Greek was only trying to put the facts in their true perspective but even so he resented it. The pain from his arm had worn away his usual calm temper and left him feeling sick and irritable. He said shortly: 'We'll manage. Someone will be out looking for us before long.'

Dorapho said no more. It was too hot to argue and the Greek shrewdly realised that the young pilot would be more reasonable once the throbbing from his arm had eased. What was left to be said could wait till then.

Only Leo Rex failed to see it the same way. 'The guy's right,' he blared loudly. 'You've got to do something better than that, son.'

Steve Navarr decided that he didn't like Rex. He hadn't thought a lot of the man from the moment he first set eyes on him, and now he was sure he was going to hate the American's guts. He said bitingly: 'Suppose he hires a six-geared camel and rides out for help and a trio of dancing girls? Will that suit your requirements?'

Rex caught the warning glint in the cynic's hard eyes. He knew instinctively that the other was losing patience and wisely refrained from answering.

Kelley said wearily: 'Come on, let's move.'

The two airmen led the way with the dark-haired Kay Leonard between them, pushing through the waist high vegetation along the jungle's edge towards another clearing that was well away from the hasty graves they had made for Larrieux and the Chinese. The rest of the party straggled along behind them, swearing and stumbling through the tangle of bush and bracken. Navarr glanced back to see Schelde struggling as he helped the little Englishwoman along. The woman had not uttered one word since the crash, and her plump, grief-twisted face was streaked with tear trails. She seemed totally uncaring and unwilling to help herself, and the little Belgian was having difficulty in holding her up. Navarr dropped back to help him and saw Lorretta de Valoise give him a curious glance as she passed. It made him wonder again what she was thinking.

'Thank you, Mr. Navarr.' Schelde sounded sincerely grateful when Navarr took hold of the woman from the other side. 'She is Mrs. Ballard. Mrs. Ruth Ballard, that is all she will tell me. Her husband is dead in the plane and she will not talk.' The little man was perspiring heavily as he spoke, his once off-white suite was now blackened with streaks of soot and sweat. His yellow tie fluttered like a wet, bedraggled banner from his neck.

He went on breathlessly: 'I think she is suffering from bad shock. She will be all right perhaps in a little while.'

Navarr saw the blank stare in the woman's eyes behind her thin-rimmed glasses, and personally doubted whether she would ever be all right again. The vacant expression and slack mouth were an ominous indication of her state of mind. Ruth Ballard's brain was more than shock-dazed, it was shattered at the very foundations.

He said evenly: 'She has taken it badly.'

Schelde nodded. 'Yes bad, very bad.'

They pushed their way through the springy sea of green to the spot that Kelley had marked as a camp site, and spent several energetic minutes trampling down the undergrowth. Then they split up into three parties, two of which were to search for food and water. Navarr and Connors went up the valley, while

Schelde and Dorapho went down. Chang Lee and the second Chinese, who, due to some mix up in his ancestry answered to the Japanese name of Asaka searched over to the far side.

While they were gone the rest gathered firewood, and despite Kay Leonard's entreaties that he should rest Kelley insisted on doing his share.

The last hours of the day passed swiftly. The sun sank lower in the western sky, tinging the distant mountains with pastel shades of deep orange and soft purple. The sky around the descending golden ball was a delicate tracery of red and yellow streaks, a compelling pattern of softly merging colour. Night was approaching fast.

Dorapho and Schelde returned to sprawl wearily upon the ground. They had found nothing eatable and no water. Dorapho could only shrug his shoulders helplessly.

A few minutes later Connors and Navarr came in, also empty handed. Kelley stared out across the darkening valley, but could seen no sign of the two Chinese. His face was grim. They had no food, no water, no shelter. It was almost night and two members of their party were still missing in the jungle.

5

The First Night

Within a very few moments the sun had completely set, the last trailing fingers of light drawing a blanket of darkness over the jungle hills as they faded from view behind the western ranges. The dense shadows of the night settled in. A breath of wind disturbed the foliage with a rustling murmur, but the air was still humid. From somewhere out in the jungle came the single, distant cry of a jackal.

Kelley said at last: 'I'll light the fire. It'll help to guide them home.' He knelt before the mound of sticks and grasses they had gathered. It flared up swiftly, throwing a pool of flickering light that showed up their anxious faces. All were watching the dark valley where Chang Lee and Asaka had disappeared.

The blonde actress said slowly: 'What

happens if they don't come back?'

Kelley answered: 'We'll give them another half hour, then Hatch and I will go and look for them.'

There was an uncomfortable silence. There was a lot that they wanted to discuss, but with the Chinese both missing and unaccounted for no one was willing to talk. They sat, or stood, around the fire, looking into the night — and hoping.

Then abruptly they heard a sound. Faint movements out in the valley that grew into the noise of heavy bodies forcing a passage through the undergrowth. Seconds later there was a shout, and the two Chinese loomed up, beaming widely, out of the night.

'Thank God!' Kelley murmured, and then ran to meet them. Connors followed him and they escorted the two men, laughing and joking, into the firelight. Chang Lee was in his shirt sleeves and carried his jacket in a bundle. Asaka was helping him and for once their inscrutable faces were wreathed in smiles. They dumped the jacket on the ground and let it fall open to reveal a mound of what looked like large spiky melons with a scattering of smaller pear-shaped fruits.

Lorretta de Valoise picked up one of the spiky fruits.

'What is it?' she asked dubiously.

'It is called dorian,' Asaka told her. 'The smell is not nice but to taste it is very good.' He borrowed the knife Kelley had taken from Larrieux and quartered a fruit for the girl.

She wrinkled her nose at the smell and a flicker of humour gleamed in Asaka's slitted eyes. Chang Lee grinned openly.

'Ugh,' she blurted. 'I can't eat this, it'll make me sick.'

Steve Navarr smiled, he had heard of the vile-smelling but sweet-tasting dorian, although he would not have known what to look for. He accepted one from Asaka, and felt something almost akin to sympathy with Lorretta as he brought it near his nose. It smelt horrible. Then he sank his teeth into the juicy flesh and was pleasantly surprised.

The two Chinese set an example by

carving some more of the fruit and eating, and soon the whole party plucked up enough courage to follow suit. The small pear-shaped fruits the Chinese had found were guavas, and although somewhat acid tasting they made a welcome dessert. The meal was juicy and helped to allay their thirst as well as their hunger.

A pale quarter moon had come up by the time they settled down to take stock of their position; tinging the foliage with dappled shades of grey and white. It passed almost unnoticed.

Leo Rex said bluntly: 'Well, son, just how long do you think it's gonna be before we're picked up?'

Kelley glared angrily at the large outline of the balding American. That word son kept prodding him like a needle on a raw nerve. He said flatly: 'I can't even guarantee that we will be picked up, let alone when.'

'Whaddaya mean by that? You guys got out a signal didn't ya? You sent an S.O.S. saying where we went down?'

Kelley shook his head. 'I can't be sure because I blacked out for a few minutes, but I don't think that a signal could have possibly been sent.'

There was a moment's lull as his words hung sombre and grim over the firelit clearing, leaving them temporarily stupefied, their faces frozen and expressionless masks in the light of the flames. Some of the bone-dry husks of bamboo began to pop and bang in the fire but no one seemed to hear them.

Then Connors said gravely: 'I saw Wall, Scott, he was cut to pieces in that first burst from the fighter. He never had a chance to get a signal out.'

Rex came to life then. 'No signal,' he said harshly. 'You guys must have sent a signal.'

Dorapho said quietly: 'I think we all believed that. This puts things in a different light.'

'You bet it does! How the hell are we gonna get outa here?'

Kelley began: 'We'll get — '

Then Lorretta de Valoise cut in tightly: 'We're going to die. That's what's going to happen. You've got to *do* something.'

Her voice was shrill, and Navarr waited

for her to break into the long burst of hysterics that he had been expecting ever since the plane crashed. It never came. Her blue eyes were staring slightly, and there was just a trace of a quiver about her mouth, she seemed to be holding herself tightly in check and Navarr felt almost disappointed. A temperamental outburst from her would have confirmed his mental summing-up of her character. And Navarr didn't like to be proved wrong.

Dorapho spoke again. 'What exactly is our position, Captain? I think you should explain — without interruption.' He looked straight at Rex as he added the last two words.

Kelley straightened his legs in an effort to get more comfortable before he began. 'Our position is pretty grim to say the least. A plane will be sent out to look for us no doubt. They won't let us disappear without a search. But the chances of a search plane finding us are pretty remote. They know the course we were following, but even in those few minutes between being attacked and coming down we veered several miles off our route. In this hilly country they could fly close by without ever spotting us.'

Connors added evenly: 'There's also the fact that we might have come down anywhere between Nakai and Hanoi, and that's a lot of country. In fact, for all they know, we might have nosedived into the Bay of Bengal and be lost for good. Our hopes of being found from the air are really too slim to worry about.'

'Well,' Rex demanded. 'What are ya gonna do?'

Kelley faced him through the flames. 'We'll walk out. It's our only hope.'

'Walk? Are you Goddamned crazy?'

Lorretta backed him up: 'I can't walk through this kind of country. I insist that we stay here and wait to be picked up.' She folded her arms across her breasts and tilted her chin upwards. 'Somebody will find us, and I'm going to wait here until they do.'

Dorapho chuckled. 'If you are wise you will do as you're told. It will be lonely here on your own.'

Navarr saw the look of surprise that

crossed the actress's features, and smiled to himself. He wouldn't have minded betting that before long she was going to regret losing Barney and the man she called Hal, who had both jumped at her every command. Miss de Valoise was heading for a long-overdue comedown.

Kelley glared them into silence, and then said flatly: 'We've already told you the position. Our chances of being picked up are practically nil. The only way to get out of this is on our own feet.'

'Without food or water, it will be difficult, very difficult.' Schelde spoke the words almost solemnly.

Kelley grimaced. 'We shall have to hunt for it as we go along. Even so we stand as good a chance of surviving as by staying here. Here we have no water either.'

Connors added: 'And remember Larrieux. There's a hell of a lot more at stake here than our own lives. There's those thousands of people back on Nakai. At least one of us has literally *got* to survive. Somebody must get back with Larrieux's report.'

Kelley said: 'This is what I've got in mind. We are down somewhere on the eastern flanks of the Arakan yomas, the forested mountain range that runs parallel with the sea on the west coast of Burma. Somewhere east of here, it can't possibly be more than a hundred miles, runs the Irrawaddy, ripping right up the length of the country. If we trek east we must eventually reach that river, and even if we don't stumble into a hill village before then, we'll find some help there, there's plenty of river traffic running up and down the Irrawaddy. We only have to make ten miles a day and we can reach it in ten days' time. Even with the women an average of ten miles a day should be possible.'

'It is very rough country, very hard going.' Schelde's fat face was regretful and he spread his hands in a vague gesture. 'Without food or water — very difficult.'

Kelley said grimly: 'Everything we plan is on the assumption that we can first find food and water.' He glanced across at the two Chinese who had been listening attentively but blandly saying nothing. 'Do you think we can find food?' he asked.

Chang Lee looked uncomfortable, he puffed out his lips and played with a single strand of his sleek black hair while he made up his mind. Then he said cautiously: 'We can find fruit. Plenty fruit in forest for those who know what to look for. But fruit bad diet to trek through jungle on. Need meat; water.'

Connors said thoughtfully: 'There's several miles of electrical wiring in the plane, with luck there'll be enough left to make some snares, and there's plenty of bird life in these hills. Our real problem is water. Unless we can find a stream or something tomorrow, we'll die of thirst.'

Kelley nodded. 'Everything hinges on our being able to find water, and some way of carrying it. We've just got to keep hoping, and pray for plenty of luck.'

Rex said harshly: 'That's all? How far do you expect to get on just hope and luck?'

'I don't know.' Kelley's tone was taut.

'You don't know! You expect us to

calmly follow you through a hundred goddamned miles of this stinking jungle. And you don't know.'

Dorapho spoke up suddenly and calmly. 'These two men are flyers, Rex. If they say that it's near impossible for us to be picked up from the air, then I guess they know their business. Therefore we can only hope that the jungle will be kind enough to let us walk out.'

The two inscrutable Chinese permitted themselves two slight nods of approval at his words. They accepted their fate with philosophical calm, observing the facts and saying nothing.

Navarr threw in a casual: 'That's a fair summing-up.' They were about the only words he had so far offered in the argument. To Navarr's mind the points in question were ones that the jungle would settle for them. Arguing was a waste of time.

There was nothing more to be said and slowly the party settled down for the night. They made up their fire, and Scott Kelley allotted each of the eight men an hour apiece to keep watch in case of prowling animal life. He took the first hour himself, while the rest of them sprawled uncomfortably around the wavering circle of firelight. The pale moon was higher now, and the lush vegetation of the valley was flecked and shadowed in its light. On the far side the jungle hills glimmered faintly as they stretched away towards the high, forested mountains. The black depths of the jungle which enclosed them on three sides were full of unsubstantial moving shapes, ghost shadows that stirred dimly in the moonlight. From afar they heard again the weird cry of a jackal, a pathetic scavenger roaming the jungle wastes to the west.

Navarr lay fully awake, unable to sleep, carefully studying his companions around the camp fire. Scott Kelley was holding his shattered arm as he sat upright before the flames on watch. Navarr realised that that arm was giving the young pilot more pain than most of them guessed. Once Kelley squeezed his eyes shut, his face grey and twisted, streaming sweat. He stayed like that for several minutes, fighting a silent battle against the onslaught of pain. Navarr found a new respect for him, and wished that there was something he could do.

His gaze moved on to rest on Ruth Ballard. Frail and weak, he doubted that she would get out alive, doubted if she even cared about living any more. His glance strayed to Lorretta de Valoise. She was carefully posed, even in this situation. She lay half on one side, her head on her arm, the open neckline of her blouse falling open to half-reveal one perfect breast. Navarr grinned and glanced at her face. In that moment he could have sworn that she had only just snapped her eyes shut.

The idea that she had been watching him filled him with a vague sense of amusement, and with that thought in mind he finally dozed off to sleep. He awoke to find Hatch Connors shaking his elbow. It was his turn to keep watch.

Navarr stood over the fire and watched the dry twigs and bamboo husks burning in the flames. The smoke was thick above the fire for it was rising straight up. It was hot and after a few minutes Navarr turned away.

He walked to the edge of the clearing that they had made, and stared down the valley. The moon was high now, and silvering the motionless river of shrub and fern. It was palely beautiful, and he wondered if a real river had ever run along here. It seemed very possible. It was a pity there wasn't one here now. He pushed his hands into his pockets and then abruptly heard a movement behind him.

It was an obvious sound. There was nothing furtive or stealthy about it. It was unhurried, too, and consequently he took his time in turning round. He faced Lorretta de Valoise.

For a moment neither of them spoke, her deep blue eyes were vaguely hesitant, and her hands smoothed her tight skirt in a self-conscious gesture. The moon gave an almost white tint to her golden hair and for the first time she seemed unsure of herself.

Unconcerned Navarr said: 'Well?'

'I wanted to ask you something — '

She stopped hesitantly. 'No, first I want to thank you for helping me out of the plane.'

So that was it. Navarr felt almost pleased. It was the only thing that explained her uncertainty, and it fitted in with her character as he saw it. Normally she would never thank anybody for anything, she would just accept it as her right. This time she felt she had to say thank you, and she didn't like it.

He said easily: 'And what was it you wanted to ask?'

She pushed the silken wave of her hair back over her shoulder. Her eyes held his face almost nervously. She said: 'Did you notice the two men who were with me — ' she faltered, then rushed on ' — the man beside me was Barney, my manager. The man behind him was his secretary, Hal. What happened to them?'

'They died, it's obvious.'

'I want to know how. I never saw — I thought — I thought perhaps you did.'

Navarr said quietly: 'Hal stopped a bullet. Barney didn't have the sense to strap himself in, he shot over the seat in front and broke his neck.'

She said abruptly: 'You're wrong you know.'

She was thinking of those last few minutes as the plane streaked earthwards, of Barney thrusting her hard into her seat and strapping the safety belt around her middle, short, complex Barney who had so many varying sides to his nature, Barney who, she was now sure, had loved her in his humble and adoring fashion. Barney who had strapped her safely to her seat, but had had no time to save himself.

She was beginning to hate herself over the way she had treated Barney.

She said again: 'You're wrong you know.' Emphasising the words curtly, her tone vicious with anger that suddenly rose against this self-certain man who could so calmly dismiss Barney as not having had the sense to strap himself in.

Navarr raised his eyebrows in a smile, half inviting her to say more. She didn't, and he wondered what the hell she really wanted. He didn't particularly like the idea of being told he was wrong without reason, either.

He said calmly: 'What do you think of the moonlight? Isn't it just the setting for making passionate love on a palm-shaded beach? Or for merely getting stinking drunk in a down-town bar?'

'I wouldn't know.'

'About the down-town bar, I suppose? I guess you'd prefer drinking highballs in a night club.'

'About either.' She clarified coldly.

Navarr wondered why the hell he was infuriating her like this. He didn't particularly want to. He went on restrainedly: 'It's a lovely night anyway — for something.'

'I hate it!' Her hands played uncomfortably with the waist of her skirt. She had asked the question that had troubled her, and now she was uncertain how to take her leave. 'I hate everything about this damned jungle. I shouldn't even be on this damned flight. I didn't ask for it.'

'No?' The intonation made it a question.

'No!' she answered. 'We were taking a private charter plane to Manila. I'm scheduled to start work on a film there about the war in the Philippines. Then the plane had engine trouble and we had to land at Nakai. This flight, and then a change at Hanoi, was our quickest way out. Now it doesn't look as if I'm ever going to get out.'

Navarr reflected that here at least was one lousy film that would never be inflicted on a long-suffering public. And then, feeling that he ought to say something cheering, he said: 'We'll get out, eventually.'

Her blue eyes might have been angry but he wasn't certain. She said coldly: 'You might, in fact I think you will. You're so damn sure of yourself that you've never considered that *you* might die. The rest of us might die by the wayside — but you'll get out.'

Navarr grinned. 'If you'll be nice to me I might even take you with me. Being nice is the right phrase in your world, isn't it?'

She stiffened. 'There's a word for you

in my world too — it starts with a capital B.'

Navarr saw the glint of fury in her eyes and the swift heave of her breasts. Her mouth was tight and angry, and her fists were clenched. In another moment she would have spun away, but the memory of the way she had harassed the unfortunates back at the airport raised a swirl of devilment within Navarr. He still felt she needed tanning but settled for the next best thing. He lunged one lean arm around her waist and drew her to him, leaning forward as she strained her head back and kissing her roughly on the mouth.

They almost fell over backwards as she writhed in his grasp. She twisted her face away, and then jerked herself free. Her blouse was heaving and her eyes were wild as she clenched one fist and drove it smack into Navarr's jaw.

The lean-faced cynic blinked, and stepped back a pace. His teeth were hurting where they had been snapped together by the impact of her fist.

He grinned insolently. 'That wasn't

very lady-like was it? A lady would have slapped, not punched.'

She punched him again, smack on the nose, then turned and strode furiously away.

Navarr stroked his nose ruefully and smiled.

6

The First Day

Navarr awoke with the dawn the next morning, but remained lazing on his back until Scott Kelley pushed himself to his feet and ordered them all into movement before the sun became too hot.

The others sat up slowly, some blinking, Rex complaining. Lorretta looked indignant, and Navarr guessed that her usual time of rising would be nearer noon. She deliberately refused to look in the tall newspaperman's direction.

Kelley split the men into two groups. Dorapho and Schelde he sent with the two Chinese to gather more fruit, the rest he led back to the wreck of the plane to see if there was anything they could possibly salvage. Lorretta and Kay were left to look after Ruth Ballard.

Kay watched the two parties move out, and then knelt by the silent woman.

128

Ruth Ballard's grey hair seemed to have become more silvery overnight. Her eyes, behind her thin spectacles, were blank. Kay said softly: 'Mrs. Ballard.'

There was no answer. No sign that she had been heard.

Lorretta repeated Kay's words. 'Mrs. Ballard, please!'

Slowly the woman looked up. She said quite evenly: 'Howard is dead isn't he?'

The two girls realised with a little shock that they were the first words she had spoken.

Kay said gently: 'I'm afraid so, Mrs. Ballard.'

Ruth Ballard looked away again. She said no more.

Kelley's party were searching vaguely around the twisted skeleton of white metal which had been the plane. The whole area was charred and blackened, the vegetation crisped to ashes. The branches on the outskirts of the fire had curled away from the fiendish heat, and now sprouted black and brittle from the backcloth of green. The warped wreckage had been flung apart by the exploding fuel tanks, and the ground was still warm.

Navarr kicked on something metallic, and glancing down saw a round shape half buried in the ashes. There was something familiar about it and he stooped to pick it up. It was the metal outer-casing of a vacuum flask. He realised that it could be used to carry a small amount of water if they ever found any, and kept it in his hand. He moved on, finding scraps of seats, jagged strips of steel, a wheel complete with rubber tyre which was still smoking. The fine ash was beginning to make him sneeze, and the gruesome portions of what had once been passengers made him feel sick.

A glimpse of blue from the surrounding vegetation caught his eye and he moved towards it. It was a canvas holdall, complete with zip and the air company's crest. His mind was still on water and he almost ran towards it. The holdall was made of canvas and could carry a lot more water than the flask casing. He pulled it out from the clump of ferns where it had landed and saw that it was intact. If he had been an excitable man he would have probably jumped for joy, for without some means of carrying water they hadn't a hope of walking out. But Navarr wasn't excitable, and he merely held out his find, and smiled.

Connors came towards him, and Navarr explained what he had in mind. The navigator grinned approvingly, and they concentrated on finding more of the canvas holdalls, for there had been one for every passenger. They found another two that were half burnt away, and then struck lucky again, another of the blue holdalls lay intact near the tail of the plane.

Twenty yards away Kelley had found part of one of the engines and with Rex's help he was stripping it of the wiring. He was still thinking of snares for trapping birds, and was determined to salvage a good supply of the electrical wire. With the help of the knife, they were managing to cut off quite usable lengths.

Connors and Navarr carried on the general search without finding much else. They collected up every piece of headgear they could find, charred or otherwise, knowing that to attempt a hatless trek through the jungle was simply asking for sunstroke. At the moment only four of them possessed any kind of a hat at all. Connors and Kay Leonard still had their uniform caps, and the two Chinese both possessed floppy, wide-brimmed, panama-type hats. The others were bare-headed.

They opened the few suitcases that had been thrown clear, but found little that would be of any use. They had to travel light, so there was no point in taking the spare clothes they found, although they did retrieve a pair of white silk nightdresses from a woman's case. The white silk would make useful bandages for Kelley's arm.

After a quarter of an hour they joined Kelley and Rex to compare finds, and found that the others had retrieved almost thirty yards of wire in varying lengths. They stood around the wreckage thoughtfully, eyeing the twisted heaps of steel and wondering if there was anything they had missed. Then Rex moved suddenly forwards and picked something up from the ground. He studied it vaguely but said nothing, his brow furrowed dubiously.

Connors said curiously: 'What is it?'

Rex turned and held out his open hand, in it lay a narrow sliver of glass from the shattered windows. 'It was just an idea.' The American's face was serious. 'I had a buddy once who used to shoot game with a bow and arrow. He took me on a trip with him up in Canada. We had special bows and steel arrows, and spent a week hunting Caribou. We even got one too.' He hesitated then went on: 'I figured we might make arrow heads outa these glass slivers. Bind 'em outa some straight bamboo with that wire you got, and use the long lengths for bow-strings. They wouldn't be any good for Caribou but we could kill birds. It's easier to be accurate when you're sighting down a long arrow than with that poky little automatic.'

For a moment they considered the idea, then Connors grinned.

'I think you've got something, Rex. That gun isn't any good, and we haven't got the ammunition to last long, anyway. But a bow is just as good if you know how to use it.'

Kelley said calmly: 'Let's hope one or two of us get the knack pretty quickly. The idea is sound, providing we can learn to use them before we starve.'

They began another slow search for any pointed slivers of window glass that could be used as arrow heads, their actions stirring up grey clouds from the ash carpet. All four were coughing huskily by the time they finished, and they retreated hastily from the scene.

Back at their camp the two girls were trying unsuccessfully to get Ruth Ballard to talk. They gave it up when they saw the first party coming back, and they got up to meet them. Lorretta glanced at the articles they had salvaged, particularly the armful of headgear that Connors carried.

'Ye Gods!' she commented. 'What are you going to do, set up a hat shop?'

Connors smiled. 'Nobody walks about the jungle without a hat. Not in this heat.'

'Well, if you think I'm going to wear one of those dirty looking things you're mistaken. Why, there's no telling who wore them last.'

Navarr laughed softly. 'You'll wear one, honey, otherwise the sun will bleach those blonde waves milk white. And your fans might not approve.'

'You're so smart you ought to be in a circus,' she snapped back. Angrily she took a step forward to inspect the hats. The cleanest was a floppy-brimmed panama. She picked it up and jammed it hard on her head. Even more angrily, she turned away.

There were three remaining panamas, one of them burnt and blackened around the brim. Navarr took the burnt one and left the others for Kelley and Rex. A feathered and veiled thing they gave to Ruth Ballard, a trilby, and a pork-pie affair, they set aside for Dorapho and Schelde.

Kelley said cheerfully: 'Well, now we've had the share-out we'd better get moving. We'll make up a couple of bows and arrows while we wait for the others to

135

bring back the breakfast.'

'Bows and arrows,' echoed Lorretta sharply. 'What the hell are you going to do now, play cowboys and Indians?'

Navarr grinned. 'Not quite. We're going to play cupids, and go around in our underwear shooting little pink hearts.'

'Shut up,' interrupted Kelley amiably. 'Navarr, you take the knife and gather some suitable wood for the bows.'

During the next hour they sorted out over a dozen perfectly straight lengths of bamboo to make arrows. Slitting one end, they inserted dagger-like splinters of glass and bound them with wire. Flights they could add when they had killed their first bird and won their feathers. They also made three long bows, strung with engine wire.

Rex bent one of the bows approvingly. 'Pretty good,' he said. 'Not like those we used Caribou hunting, but they should serve us pretty well when it comes to birds.'

Lorretta pouted. 'Isn't it just my luck! I get involved in a crash aboard a plane

I shouldn't have been on, and end up in the company of a lot of little boys who want to play bows and arrows.'

'What would you prefer?' asked Navarr. 'Mothers and Fathers — or should it be just good friends?'

At that point their four companions returned with two jackets full of fruit, which the Chinese had again discovered, and the arrival of breakfast terminated the argument.

Swiftly one of the two piles of fruit was shared out. Dorians were again the bulk of the meal, but this time there were no up-tilted noses at their evil smell. Even Lorretta was obviously grateful as she bit into the juicy flesh. The tasty, pulp-covered, seeds of some pomegranates Asaka had found made a passable dessert. Soon several eyes were straying over to the second pile of fruit, as yet untouched.

Deliberately Kelley covered it up, handling it clumsily with one hand as he placed it deep in the shade. He straightened up and told them quietly, 'Right, now we've got to search for water, and we shall probably need those a lot more when we get back. I think the best thing is for the men to split into four parties of two and take different directions. I'll leave the automatic with Kay and the moment a party returns having found water she can fire a signal to bring the others back. While we're at it, each pair can take a bow and a couple of arrows. If we get a shot at any kind of game we might as well be prepared to take it.'

Connors said flatly: 'You'd better stay with the women, Scott. You won't help that arm by barging about in the jungle.'

Kelley's face hardened. 'The arm will be okay. It doesn't stop me from walking. I might as well do something useful as sit here feeling sorry for myself.'

No one else argued, and the men split into pairs. Navarr found himself with Chang Lee, crossing the valley and climbing the far ridge to the west. Lorretta watched him go, recalling his brutal kiss and wondering why she felt a strange attraction to the man. The logical thing to do was to hate him.

Ruth Ballard didn't look up as the men

moved out. She sat silent and still, her mind clinging to the treasured memory of her husband's face, Howard's kindly, ageing face with its slightly reproving smile. She had to hold that picture, had to keep it forever in her mind, clinging to it with every fibre of her being. For when she didn't, another picture took its place; a pain-ravaged Howard, his face twisted in agony as the sky pirate swooped in to rake the airliner with murderous fire.

She couldn't bear that second face.

On the far side of the valley, Navarr was leading the way with Chang Lee at his heels. The going was tough and the ridge rose steeply. The trees were choked with ferns and brambles. Leafy branches twined with slender spearheads of wavering bamboo. Overhead a blanket of greenery shut out the sky. The air was humid, sucking the perspiration from their flesh. The bird life was abundant but kept on the move, never offering a reasonable bow shot.

They kept on for half an hour before Navarr signalled breathlessly for a rest. Without speaking they wearily subsided into sitting positions on the hillside and faced each other. Chang Lee's face was shiny and deeply shadowed under his hat. He managed a slow grin, his gold teeth looking dull in the gloom. He took off his hat and smoothed his slick hair.

Navarr said casually: 'You said you worked in Viet Nam once, what did you do there?' He asked more because he felt he ought to attempt some sort of conversation rather than out of curiosity.

Chang smiled. 'I work for big cotton corporation; agent who goes from one field to another. Once I was manage plantation in Viet Nam. Jungle is much alike all over Asia, and what you learn in one country is useful in another. In Viet Nam I often eat the fruits I have recognise here.'

Navarr grinned. 'Good job too! Without you the rest of us would have starved by now.'

'Thank you.' The Chinese sounded almost uncomfortable.

After a short rest they moved on again, moving steadily up the jungle-flanked hillside. The terrain was the same all the way up, and only occasionally did they cross a small clearing where there was no need to force a passage or duck through trailing vines. In these clearings there were sometimes clumps of orchids or bushes of Jasmine, creating colourful splashes against the background of infinite green.

It took them two hours of alternately climbing and pausing for short breathers before they finally gained the top of the ridge. The sun was high and they were wet with sweat, the heat lay like a close, steamy blanket all around them. They had to move along the hilltop before they found a fairly clear space where they could look down into the next valley. There was nothing but more jungle and another ridge rising beyond; and behind that was the dark outlines of yet another ridge. There was no sign of water.

Chang Lee had to swallow once or twice before he found the breath to speak. He declared slowly: 'There might be water beneath the trees. To find out we must go down.'

Navarr grimaced. 'Okay, so we'll go

down.' He led the way.

However only disappointment awaited them at the bottom, there was no stream flowing along the valley floor. It was obvious that any stream entering the valley above them would have to come this way, so now their only course was to move down the valley and hope to find water below.

They struggled on gamely. The sun rose ever higher until several hours later Chang tripped and fell flat on his face. Navarr picked him up, realising grimly that they had to turn back. There was no water in this valley, and it was too late to attempt to explore the one beyond. Wearily they retraced their steps the way they had come.

Once the Chinese stopped by a smooth-stemmed citrus tree and plucked a few small green limes. They were too young, sour and bitter, but the tangy juice helped to combat their thirst, and they filled their pockets before pushing on.

The climb up the ridge to get back to their own valley left them exhausted and they collapsed weakly among a thicket of waist-high bracken at the top. The green-brown ferns swayed above them as they waited to build up another reserve of strength, their serrated fronds creating strange notched shadows in the sun. Then abruptly they heard a shot.

It came sharp and clear from the valley below and it took them several minutes to realise what it meant. Then the echoes spelt out one word. Water. One of the search parties had found water.

Both men sprang to their feet. That one shot had revived them better than anything else could have done. Willingly they plunged down the ridge into the dense jungle. They emerged three hours later, drenched in sweat with their clothes snagged in a thousand places. The waist-high river of green that ran through their own valley almost brought them to a standstill, but finally they staggered weakly into camp.

Only Schelde and Asaka had yet to return. Connors and Rex had brought their holdall back full to the zip with water. The successful pair had struck out up the east ridge and encountered much the same kind of terrain as Navarr and Chang Lee had done. They, too, had been disappointed when they reached the crest of the ridge, but had descended into the valley in the same hope of finding a stream hidden by overhanging jungle. At the bottom they had almost fallen into a narrow ravine where a thin trickle of water coursed along the valley floor. Thankfully they had drunk all they needed, and then filled the holdall, hurrying back as fast as they could go.

Navarr and Chang Lee drank much-needed cupfuls of water as they listened to Connors's story. The cups had been supplied by Kay, who realising that they had nothing to drink from, had made a lone trip to the plane and had been lucky enough to find two tops from some shattered vacuum flasks.

As they finished drinking Schelde and Asaka came in. The Chinese was grinning broadly and was holding aloft a pair of plump, dark-brown birds that looked like pheasants. Schelde explained that having heard the shot and realising that one party had already found water, he and Asaka had concentrated on hunting game. More by persistence than skill they had succeeded, for they had missed a dozen sitting targets for each bird they dropped.

Rex grinned widely as they told their story, and Navarr half expected him to point out that the bows and arrows had been his idea. However Rex made no comment, and Navarr felt vaguely disappointed. Nobody was coming up to his expectations any more.

It was now late afternoon and the more rested male members of the party set out to gather wood. Schelde plucked the two birds and then handed them over to Kay Leonard for cleaning. Navarr watched her, for he was still regaining his breath from his dash down the ridge. Her eyes were intent on her work, and her short hair was pushed neatly under her cap. Her uniform jacket hung open, and the smooth flesh above and below her black lace bra was slightly moist, golden brown. Navarr thought that perhaps he ought to get her a blouse from the scattered luggage around the plane — she needed something to replace the one she had used on Kelley's arm — then he decided that she looked better without one.

An hour later the sun sank beyond the wild mountain crests, waving trailing banners of red cloud in a slow farewell. Hatch Connors set the watches for the night, deliberately leaving Kelley out. The co-pilot's face seemed to be ageing by the hour with the pain of his shattered arm, his will-power was finally beginning to collapse and he did not argue as Connors took over. The navigator announced calmly that they would start to trek east first thing in the morning, filling up with water at the stream he and Rex had discovered.

Navarr listened silently as he stared into the fire. He was thinking suddenly of Larrieux. The dead man's face seemed to hover ghost-like in the smoky flames. The features were sweat-glistening, pain-twisted. The thin lips moved again.

'At least one of you must survive!'
One must survive!

7

The First Deaths

Dawn found Navarr kneeling on the edge of a slightly less dense patch of the jungle hillside. He had a bamboo arrow already notched on the string of his bow, and an angled ray of sunlight glinted on the jagged sliver of glass that made the point. For almost half an hour he waited there, feeling pleasantly cool in the deep shade. Birds eyed him curiously, tiny pea-green parrots with unblinking eyes, and other varieties that moved like coloured smoke swirls through the green foliage. All were too small to tempt him into shooting. They moved confidently through the leafy maze, as if contemptuous of his ability with a long bow. Then suddenly he spotted a larger bird.

It was the size of a large chicken, and appeared to be some kind of wild turkey. It sat on a branch not twenty yards away, its dark brown colouring merging into the gloom. Navarr wondered how long it had been there as he cautiously raised his bow. Something that was almost excitement trembled through him as he sighted along the bamboo arrow. He had a clear shot. The bird was a sitting target. He just couldn't miss.

He fired and missed by a yard.

He spent a sour half-hour in hunting for his arrow, and when he found it he started back moodily. He had been gone a good hour and as the others meant to start moving it was best that he returned. On the way he saw a second bird.

It was almost as large as the first, watching him coldly from a background of foliage approximately the same distance away. Navarr was almost inclined to ignore it rather than have to search for another arrow, but his conscience intervened. Carefully he fitted the arrow to his bow. The bird watched him with interest. He took even longer over aiming this time, wondering with one vacant part of his mind what the hell the stupid bird must be thinking. Then he fired. The bird let out a startled screech and toppled to the earth.

Navarr was already bounding forwards when the bird began to run. The bamboo arrow had pierced it through the left wing and it scuttled swiftly away, uttering shrieking cries as it went. Navarr kept it in sight, his long legs stretching in great leaps as he crashed through the jungle. Every few yards the trailing arrow would snag in the undergrowth and drag the bird to a halt before it could struggle free, and in those seconds Navarr would close in only to have the bird race away again. Once he clubbed at it with his bow and missed. Then he realised that the bow was hampering him as much as the arrow hampered the bird and he threw it aside.

Branches and brambles whipped at his legs as he plunged frantically on, and then the arrow caught in some grass tufts and stopped the bird again. Navarr saw it jerk itself free while he was still yards behind and flung himself forward in a racing dive. He landed almost on top of the screaming, terrified bundle of feathers.

The impact winded him but he hung on, feeling the warm body squirming out of his hands. His fingers slipped and then closed in a firm grip around one leg. The bird screeched in terror, flailing its wings, feathers flying in all directions.

Navarr retained his hold while he got his breath back, and then, almost reluctantly, he broke the fluttering creature's neck. There was something vaguely shameful in executing such a worthy opponent. The dead bird eyed him in solemn reproach and he found himself wishing that it had closed its eyes to die.

He retraced his steps through the jungle, recovering his bow and the remainder of his arrows. The bird in his hand was heavy and a type of turkey similar to the first bird he had seen. Navarr felt pleased with it if not with himself.

Back at the camp he found that Connors and Asaka had returned empty-handed, but Rex had shot a pair of sizeable pigeons. The American admitted that he had become fairly competent with a bow while sharing his archer friend's hunting trip. Chang Lee and his party returned with more pomegranates and guavas.

They made a light breakfast on the fruit, and then, despite protests from Rex and Lorretta who still persisted in believing that they must be picked up from the air, they started off on the route that Connors and Rex had followed the previous day.

Connors led the way with Kelley close behind him. Schelde was once again helping Ruth Ballard along, while Kay Leonard helped him to steady her. Navarr saw, slightly to his disappointment, that the air hostess was wearing a cotton blouse beneath her blue uniform jacket. He later discovered that Connors had had the same thought as himself about retrieving one from the luggage about the plane, but, the navigator had done something about it.

They looked an ill-assorted crowd as they pushed their way up the jungle-covered ridge. The crude assortment of headgear, some of it partially burnt, gave them the appearance of a troupe of clowns. Schelde was wearing the pork-pie affair and it balanced clumsily above his round spectacled face. Dorapho was wearing the trilby, tilted well back, and if his pitted cheeks had not marred his smile, he would have looked like a semi-negro comedian with his dark skin and short curling hair.

It took them nearly an hour and a half to force a passage up to the top of the ridge, the male members of the party taking it in turn to break a trail through the twisted foliage. The steep incline and soft soil might have made them slide backwards but for the abundance of bush and shrub, which although it hindered progress at least gave them a firm foothold. The sun climbed higher as they ascended, and soon they were again sweating freely, perspiration trickling down their faces and bodies. Several times Lorretta de Valoise fell in her high-heeled shoes, and by the time they stopped to rest on the crown of the hill she was almost in tears.

They each took a long drink while

they rested, for with the stream running through the next valley there was no need yet to ration themselves. It was after they left the stream that they would have to limit their drinking. The canvas holdalls were proving acceptable, although clumsy, water bags.

Lorretta removed her shoes and massaged her ankles as she leaned back against the bole of a tree. Her pale blue costume was dirty and her gold-tinged stockings were sadly laddered. She looked far from being the same impeccable beauty who had stepped aboard the plane at Nakai, but at the moment she was past caring. She closed her eyes, relaxing as far as it was possible to relax in the sweltering heat. Her mind strayed back to Barney and Hal and all the other males who had revolved around her as she threw scene after scene, knowing that her box-office allure made her too valuable for them to slap her as she deserved. She missed them, yet at the same time she was glad that they were not here. In the same vein of thought she resented Navarr, but was glad of his presence.

It was the instinct for self survival, for deep inside herself she knew that Navarr was the kind of man who would survive, and almost subconsciously she was glad he was there.

She thought again of Barney, wondering at the strangely complex character of the man. Weak, spineless, little Barney, who had suddenly and roughly strapped her into her seat on the plane, and in so doing had lost his chance to take similar safety precautions for himself. She felt that she would never understand Barney, and in a way his death had changed her. She would never want to harass a man for the sheer devilment of it again, just in case he proved to be another Barney. She didn't want ever to feel again that heavy feeling of guilt.

When they moved, Scott Kelley was the first man on his feet.

'Let's go,' he ordered shortly. 'It'll be past noon by the time we reach that stream. We'll stop there for a meal before pushing on.' He turned and led the way down the eastern flank of the ridge.

Dorapho helped Lorretta to her feet,

and she put her shoes on reluctantly.

'In a week or two this will all be a memory.' The Greek encouraged her. 'Try to think of it that way.'

She didn't answer as they followed the rest of the party down the ridge.

The terrain was unchanging. The whole of this part of Burma, from what Navarr recalled of his geographical knowledge, was an endless series of ridges and valleys running from the north to the south. He wondered how many times they would have to climb up and down the jungle-clad hills before they finally found a native village, or, if they couldn't find one, until they reached the broad Irrawaddy, anything up to a hundred miles away.

He began to consider their chances. It would probably take them much longer than Kelley seemed to think to cross these endless ridges and valleys. It could be done of course, but they would need time and luck and he doubted whether they would all make it. The weaker ones would fall by the wayside, and slow them down. Ruth Ballard would be one. The actress, who looked liable to fall and wrench an ankle at any moment on her high heels, would probably make the second. Schelde did not look particularly fit, and Kelley could not keep going indefinitely without cracking up. He began to wonder seriously how many of them would make it.

He wondered, too, whether they would make it in time for the warning they carried for the dead Frenchman to be of any use. He could only hope that there would be delays in the plans of the man called Voron; delays that would amount to a week or two at least. There was no telling how long the plane, in which Voron's henchman would eventually hide his deadly parcel, would stay on the ground. The communist would have no control over that, and he would have to wait until the plane was taking off before he could detonate his nuclear parcel to the best effect. To explode it on the ground would limit the blast, and leave no one who could say what had actually happened. Whereas if it went up in the air there would be distant survivors who could spread the propaganda story that one of America's own planes had exploded on take-off. Navarr had been on Nakai long enough to know that the arrival and departure of the great gleaming bombers were still regarded with awe by the islanders. The sound of an engine was still a signal to stop work and watch. One or two of them were sure to survive to tell the story as Voron wanted it told.

For the rest of the day they struggled gamely on, climbing three of the endless ridges and descending into three of the lush valleys. In the first valley they filled the canvas holdalls from the stream Connors had found. The water was fast and clear and Kelley decided that as it could not have come far it was unlikely to be infected by bacteria. In the next valley they rested again and then carried on until late afternoon. All of them were weary, but Lorretta and Ruth Ballard were the most seriously affected, Lorretta because her high heels made her ankles ache, the older woman because her age was telling.

Scott Kelley had lasted well during the day but now his resistance began to wane, his face was pale and lined. A ghost was riding Kelley all the way, the ghost of the big grey-haired pilot who had died bringing the plane down. Big Jim Rayburn had given his life for his crew and passengers, and Kelley knew he couldn't do less than that. The memory of Rayburn was the spur that helped him fight down the throbbing agony of his smashed arm.

At last it was Connors who called a halt as they breasted the crown of the third ridge. Soon it would be dark and he knew they had to prepare for the night.

Kelley gave his friend a resentful stare, then common sense intervened, and temporarily he relinquished command. He thought that they had just about covered their hoped-for average of ten miles since leaving the valley where the plane had crashed, and he felt reasonably satisfied.

They trampled down enough undergrowth to make a small clearing on the hill top, and then the three women were left to the task of cleaning the two plump pigeons Rex had shot, while the men gathered firewood. The large turkey that Navarr had brought back they meant to save for the morning.

Scott Kelley moved away from the others, gathering dry sticks as best he could with one arm. He heard the sounds of his companions crashing through the undergrowth in their search for wood but he could see no one. The jungle here was dense, and the growing dusk made it difficult to see. He wandered farther afield, down the slope of the ridge towards the next valley. Putting down his arm-load at intervals he added to it, working grimly despite his useless right arm. Kelley bitterly resented that incapability, for it prevented him from taking full charge in the way he believed that he should.

The camp clearing was lost behind him in the thick gloom, and although he could still hear the voices of his companions he knew that he was moving too far away. He turned and started back, for it was one of his own rules that no one should

159

stray away from the camp at night, it was too easy to become lost in the jungle. He had his bundle of firewood tucked under his left arm, and his right folded against his chest in the sling. He was using his feet to push aside the undergrowth and then it happened. The vegetation beneath him gave way abruptly and plunged him down into a hidden ravine. He yelled in alarm, scattering his firewood as he flailed for a grip with his good arm. He crashed heavily down the steeply sloping lip of the ravine and then found a grip as his feet shot through the restraining undergrowth into space.

He hung there with one hand, kicking out to find a foothold with his toes. His shattered arm was bleeding where he had knocked it when falling, and the pain sent him half crazy. Somehow he hung there, not realising that he was screaming almost hysterically for help.

Hatch Connors heard the screams of his friend, and charged through the darkened jungle in a blind run. It was almost pitch black now for the sun was setting swiftly. He followed the sound of Kelley's voice and forced himself to slow down as he got close.

'Scott! Scott, where are you?'

'Be — be careful — steep drop — ' Kelley's words reached him vaguely through the darkness and he moved on, feeling the ground slope sharply as he started down the lip of the ravine. He could hear Kelley close ahead of him now, the young pilot had stopped yelling and was moaning in pain. Connors moved down fast but cautiously, hanging on to the undergrowth to stop himself falling.

He saw Kelley hanging just below him and swung his body down into the mouth of the ravine. He found some footholds and got his feet firmly anchored before reaching down one arm and hooking it around Kelley's waist. They hung together over the drop into the ravine and for a moment Connors feared that Kelley had passed out.

'Scott! Scott!' he hissed sharply. 'Can you climb up with my help?'

'I don't — think so.' Kelley was leaning heavily on the navigator's arm. The pain from his shattered limb was making him weak and sick.

'Hang on,' Connors gasped. 'One of the others will be here any minute.' As he spoke he heard a rustling in the bushes above and saw a dark shape coming down the steep slope towards them. Relief flooded his frame and then abruptly died. He saw the steel blade of a knife glint in the newcomer's hand and then the keen edge chopped down viciously on to his fingers where he hung on with one hand. Connors screamed as the biting impact of the steel blade snapped his fingers open, and then Kelley's weight tore him out into space and they plunged together into the hundred foot drop to the floor of the ravine.

Their killer melted silently away into the gloom of the jungle depths.

8

A New Fear

Navarr and Dorapho arrived at the same moment, almost colliding as they crashed wildly and from different directions through the jungle barrier. Navarr saw the break in the undergrowth where Kelley had rolled into the ravine, it was barely visible in the darkness and he almost followed the two airmen over the edge before he stopped. He yelled a warning to the Greek and grabbed the man's arm, halting him at the top of the slope. They stood there panting, staring dumbly into the blackness where the broken vegetation ended.

The remaining members of the party converged rapidly on the spot, running at first and then moving cautiously when Navarr and Dorapho warned them of what was ahead. Kay Leonard attempted to push closer to the edge of the drop but the Greek held her back.

'Scott? Hatch? Where are you?' Her voice was a scream that echoed through the trees and trailed off in a despairing sob.

Dorapho said tensely: 'They must have gone over the edge.'

'Scott? . . . Hatch?' She shrieked their names again.

There was no answer.

The echoes of her cries rang tauntingly through the jungle gloom, resounding and then dying in the black depths.

Dorapho said grimly: 'I think you must face it. They are dead.'

'No! No! They — they must be just unconscious. Just unconscious, that's all.' She gripped the Greek's arms, staring wildeyed into his pitted face. 'Go down there please? Go down and help them?'

Dorapho hesitated and then said softly: 'In the pitch darkness it would be madness to climb down there.'

'Please, Mr. Dorapho, please?'

'I am sorry. If it were daylight. Or if I could hope that they lived — ' He shrugged his shoulders helplessly. 'I am sorry.'

Kay turned away from him, her mouth trembling, despair and anguish creasing the white blurr of her face. 'Mr. Navarr,' she appealed to the tall cynic. 'Please Mr. Navarr, please go down . . . ?'

Navarr glanced around the small group that clustered on the lip of the ravine, and then over to where the glimmer of their camp fire was showing through the trees. He said calmly: 'Schelde, go and get me a burning brand from the fire.'

Schelde gaped at him for a moment, and then hurried to obey. When he returned Navarr took the flaming branch from him and keeping a firm grip on the undergrowth with his free hand he climbed down the lip of the ravine. For a moment he stood on the very edge, the flame illuminating the hard set of his lean face as he stared into space. Then he tossed the burning brand into the ravine.

They watched the twisting flame fall, down and down, growing smaller and smaller. It was burning well and lasted for several seconds until the rush of air faded it to a glimmer. The branch itself glowed a dull red and finally vanished as it hit the bottom. It had fallen a good hundred feet.

Navarr climbed up slowly, steeling himself to face the look in Kay Leonard's eyes. He said quietly: 'You saw it fall. You can see how deep it is. They couldn't live through a fall like that. And it would be suicidal to try and climb down at night.'

'But they might have lived — might be just unconscious.' She saw no hope in Navarr's face and turned again. 'Mr. Rex? Mr. Schelde? Asaka . . . ' Her voice trailed off and suddenly she was sobbing. She stood there helplessly, until Lorretta gently put her arms around her and led her away.

The others followed her back to the fire-lit clearing, and stood around awkwardly. Lorretta made the air hostess sit down and sat with her, saying nothing, just keeping one firm, friendly arm about the crying girl's shoulders. Navarr watched and for the first time admitted to himself that there might be something more substantial beneath the spoilt exterior of the temperamental actress. For Navarr it was a big admission, for the tall cynic hated to find his judgement proved wrong.

For a while there was a grim silence around the camp fire, then Dorapho stood up slowly.

'I think it is best that we sleep now,' he said, his tone only slightly hesitant. 'There is nothing we can do now except think of ourselves. We will start as early as possible tomorrow, for it will be coolest at dawn.'

Rex glared resentfully at the way the Greek was taking charge. However, as the man set the watches and the others nodded in agreement, he held back and nodded sourly. Navarr watched and smiled. Rex, he decided, would like to have taken charge himself, only not having the qualities of a leader he settled for resenting those who did.

As for Navarr himself, he had no particular desire to be a leader. As long as there was someone else to carry on he was quite content to shelve the responsibility. Navarr had been a lone wolf too long to welcome the idea of people clamouring about him for leadership. He preferred to stay as he was.

The long, dismal night passed slowly, and at dawn Navarr announced that as it was now daylight he intended to descend the ravine and retrieve the knife and automatic from Kelley's body. Despite the risk the knife was something they could not do without.

Dorapho said hesitantly: 'All right, Mr. Navarr, but be careful. We can't afford to lose another man.'

Navarr grinned. 'I'm always careful.' He saw Kay Leonard watching him then and quietly promised her that he would cover the two airmen decently at the same time. She choked over her thanks and her eyes misted again. Helplessly, Navarr turned away, and began to search along the ravine's edge for a way down.

He had to follow the ravine for several hundred yards before he finally found a way, and it was some time before he reached the inert bodies of the two airmen. Glancing up he saw the others watching him from above.

He found Kelley sprawling face down, his neck was broken and there was blood staining his fair hair. Connors had landed over a rock nearby, facing the sky, his back cruelly broken.

Grimly Navarr searched them both, retrieving the knife and automatic. He took their few personal possessions as well, wristwatches, wallets and some photographs; those things the air hostess might like to keep.

There was a small hollow nearby and he placed the two friends in it side by side. It was when he went to pick up Connors that he saw the deep stain in the sand beneath the Navigator's blood-smeared hand.

The hand was outstretched, palm uppermost. Navarr turned it over and stared at the deep gash that ran across the back of the fingers, lying the flesh open to the bone. Something seemed to stop inside him as the truth dawned; that cut could not have been caused by the fall, it had been made by a knife. Kelley and Connors had been murdered.

Navarr knelt there a long time, studying the tell-tale gash across the back of Connors's hand. He could visualise quite clearly the way the two airmen had died: Connors supporting his injured friend with one hand and hanging on with the other, and then the killer slashing at his hand to make him release his hold.

In accepting the obvious fact that it was murder, Navarr had an even grimmer thought to face. Someone amongst their own party had to be the murderer. There was no one else around. But who? And why?

Slowly Navarr covered the two bodies with branches and rocks to keep the jackals at bay. Then he stood back and repeated the few words he had heard Kelley say over Larrieux.

When he had finished he looked up. His companions were standing bareheaded along the edge of the ravine, and savage anger burned within him as he saw them replace their hats. One of those solemn mourners was a hypocrite and murderer, someone who could kill in cold blood.

Navarr started back up the valley as those at the top turned away, leading Kay Leonard between them. As an afterthought he retrieved Kelley's shoes and took them with him. Kelley's feet were the smallest, and his shoes would be a relief to Lorretta from her crippling high heels. He felt that Kelley would have been the first to approve.

The climb up the ravine was much stiffer than the one down, for coming down it had been possible to slither most of the way, breaking his fall only when he gathered too much speed. Now he had to haul himself up. Shrubs and rock outcrops made plentiful hand-holds, but even so the sweat was pouring off him as he reached the top. He felt dizzy from his exertions and was glad to sprawl limply in the undergrowth above the ravine.

Here he began to consider his position. So far he alone knew that the two airmen had been murdered, and by viewing the problem rationally he could see only two courses of action. He could keep quiet and hope to lull the killer into a sense of false security, where he might later give himself away, or, he could confront the others with what he knew, and make a snap search for the murder weapon. However, the killer would have had plenty of time to get rid of the knife by now, and the latter course would only put him on his guard. That last thought, together with the fact that Navarr had never been the kind to share his problems, made up his mind for him. He would say nothing for a few hours and then make a sudden search. With luck, the murderer would have been fooled into thinking that he had noticed nothing amiss and might have taken a chance on retrieving his knife, for in their position a knife was too valuable an asset deliberately to throw away.

Slowly Navarr made his way back to the camp. Here Kay Leonard managed to thank him awkwardly, but almost broke down as he handed her the articles he had taken from the dead bodies. He took care to refrain from studying his companions too closely from then on, as Dorapho gave the order to break camp. No one disputed the Greek's words. Not even

Rex. There was an air of tragedy about this particular camp and they were none of them desirous to remain.

They picked up their bows, water bags, and the remains of the food, and with Dorapho in the lead moved out. On Navarr's suggestion they followed the same direction that he had taken along the edge of the ravine, and after just over half a mile reached a point where the ravine was shallow enough for them to descend and climb up the far side.

Lorretta was wearing the shoes that Navarr had taken from the dead pilot and had left her own high heels behind. The shoes were a little large, but by padding the toes with soft, dry moss she had made them fit and they were a lot more comfortable than her own, and no longer was she liable to wrench an ankle with every step.

Kay walked desolately beside her, dry-eyed now but her pleasant features still stained with tears. She was thinking of Scott and Hatch and how they had determined to carry on after big Jim Rayburn had died. Something of that spirit was passing into her now, a stirring legacy willed to her by the dead members of her crew.

She could see them all clearly as she walked: Wallis, a faraway look in his eyes as he thought of the girl back home, Rayburn who always smiled and referred to them as 'Children', Kelley with his boyish grin and quick laugh, Connors with a glass in his hand, gaily pouring it 'down the hatch'. She felt that they were watching her, their gaze expectant and confident. The feeling steadied her, and brought back her self-control and will-power. She wasn't going to let them down.

At the head of the column Navarr had taken over from the Greek, forcing his way grimly through the monotonous and never-ending barrier of the jungle. The tall trees overhead were again shutting out the sun, but the air was humid and sapping the moisture from their skins as always. Parrots and clusters of tiny white egrets filled the branches and kept up a careless cacophony of sound. Once something heavy started up in the undergrowth ahead and crashed away into the distance.

They rested often but made good progress until noon when Dorapho called them to a halt. The Greek took on the task of sharing out what was left of their food and issued them with half a cup of water apiece.

Rex glowered sullenly. 'How the hell do you expect us to march on one Goddamned mouthful of water? Fill the cup up.'

Dorapho eyed him coldly. The thick black stubble that was pushing through his cheeks gave him a dangerous look that belied his nature. 'We have to limit ourselves as much as we can,' he said. 'We don't know how long it will be before we find water again to refill the bags.'

'I still say fill the cup up, we've got plenty as yet. Who the heck are you to give orders anyway?'

Dorapho ignored the last sentence. He said tightly: 'We make the water last as long as we can.'

'Aw to hell with that!' Rex started to get up.

'Sit down, Mr. Rex,' Kay Leonard ordered quietly.

Rex relaxed as they turned to face her. She was calmer now, her eyes red-rimmed but steady. She said: 'We've got a long way to go, we may need that water much more later on.'

No one else spoke. After a few minutes she stood up slowly and waited for them to pack up and move. Dorapho led the way eastwards up the next ridge.

They crossed another two ridges during the afternoon, and an hour before sundown Dorapho halted them for the night. They rested wearily before using the last hour of daylight to set up camp.

Dorapho, Navarr, Asaka, and Rex, each took a bow and moved into the jungle to hunt while the others gathered wood.

Navarr wandered about hopefully with an arrow notched in his bow, but nothing worth while came into range. At last the shadows began to gather and he returned to camp. Dorapho had insisted that they all returned before dusk, and his reasoning was sound.

He found that Rex alone had managed to kill a small type of quail and that Kay Leonard was already turning it on a rough spit. The air hostess had her grief well under control now, but there was still a look of desolation in her hazel eyes. She had loved both Kelley and Connors like a pair of unruly brothers, and she knew that had they lived she would have eventually married one of them. She didn't know which one, but now it hardly mattered. She only knew that their loss had left an irreparable vacuum in her heart.

Navarr sat down and watched the girl work, admiring the way she had pulled herself round. Then Chang Lee interrupted his thoughts by saying brusquely:

'Where is Mr. Asaka?'

For the first time Navarr realised that the bland-faced Chinese was not present. Everyone else was there, but not Asaka.

Dorapho said slowly: 'He was gathering wood.' He stood up and called the man's name loudly. They waited as his voice died slowly away, but there was no answer.

Navarr remembered how Kelley and Connors had died and was filled with sudden fear. He said sharply: 'We'd better look for him.'

Dorapho called the Chinese again. The echoes faded. 'Okay,' the Greek decided. 'But everybody be careful. Watch where you are going.'

The five men split up in different directions: moving slowly through the jungle and calling the missing Chinese. Kay and Lorretta searched with them, keeping close together in the gloom. Only Ruth Ballard remained in the fire-lit camp.

Navarr felt grimly responsible as he forged through the jungle. He was haunted by a new fear that there was a maniac among them, and he had let Asaka go into the jungle unwarned. His palms were sweating and the moisture was running out from between his clenched fists. A branch whipped at his face but he hardly felt it. He called Asaka's name as he moved farther away from the camp. Each time he shouted he paused and listened for an answer. He was only half aware of the fact that his companions were getting farther away and that for the moment he was alone in the dense tangles of the jungle. He shouted, then paused, shouted and paused again. He heard a sharp clicking sound from behind him as he listened and instinct made him throw himself abruptly sideways.

A slender shaft of bamboo zipped past his shoulder as he moved and arched into the gloom beyond.

Navarr lay sweating in the dank undergrowth. He heard a slight rustling from somewhere behind him, but no more. Slowly he got to his feet and went forward to retrieve the arrow. It was one of their own, deadly, tipped with a jagged point of glass. It had been meant for him.

The new fear was confirmed then. He stood in the darkness, silent and still, holding the murderous shaft in his hands. Someone had tried to kill him, and it was obvious now that Asaka was not coming back. Somebody was out to kill them all. One of their number was a maniac.

9

One River to Cross

There was no doubt in Navarr's mind as he made his way slowly back to the clearing. The rest of the party were re-gathering in the firelight, and he waited until they had all returned before saying grimly:

'Asaka isn't coming back. He's dead.'

They looked at him slowly, disbelieving, the words seemed to stun them into silence, and then Dorapho asked:

'How? How did he die?'

'He was murdered. I can't be more definite than that because I haven't found his body. But I know he was murdered.'

'Say, what is this?' Rex sounded nervous.

Navarr glanced around at their shocked expressions, expressions that were shadowed and warped by the flickering glow of the flames. They could have meant anything.

He said: 'Both Kelley and Connors were murdered too. When I turned Connors over I found a deep gash across the back of his hand; a knife cut. Somebody almost cut his fingers off while he was holding Kelley and hanging on to the edge of that ravine with one hand. That's how they died. Tonight Asaka vanishes and doesn't return. And then — ' he held out the bamboo arrow ' — then somebody just fired this at me. If it hadn't clicked on a branch while in flight it would have hit me smack in the back. It all adds up to one answer. We've got a killer amongst us; a maniac.'

Navarr stopped, watching their faces, trying to read something in the tight lines of their features. In the smoky half-light it was impossible to get a proper impression. Only Kay Leonard's face seemed clear, staring, horrified. Navarr felt mean and rotten at having thrown the facts of the two airmen's murders in her face. But it had to be that way. He had to try and force a reaction from their killer. Only he had failed. They all looked the same.

Dorapho said at last: 'If this is true, about the airmen, why did you not say so before?'

'There were good reasons,' Navarr answered. 'Whoever killed Kelley and Connors had a knife. A knife that he's been keeping hidden from the rest of us. When he realised that I meant to go down into the ravine he would have disposed of the knife, for if it was found on him it would prove him a murderer. So I said nothing, hoping that he would believe that I had not noticed the cut on Connors's hand. If I could make him believe that then it was possible he would recover the knife. I meant to search all of you later after he had had time to retrieve it. I think it's time I made that search now.'

There was silence. The crackle of the fire sounding vaguely sinister and filling the clearing.

Dorapho spoke first. 'I think it is best you search. You will search me first.'

Without comment Navarr ran his

hands over the Greek. He checked the man thoroughly, satisfying himself that Dorapho had no concealed knife on his person. Schelde moved forward, his short arms out-stretched, his eyes looking almost hurt behind his glasses. He had no knife either.

Rex said angrily: 'Nobody's gonna search me. I just ain't standing for it.'

Navarr said coldly: 'I'm searching you. Whether you're on your feet or flat on your back makes no difference.'

'Are you threatening me? How do we know it ain't you? You might be doing all this just to fool us. I wanna search you too.'

'You can do that.' Navarr began to run his hands over the American's clothing. Rex fumed but made no attempt at resistance.

Chang Lee submitted to the process without comment. Then Navarr allowed Rex to search him in his turn. No knife was found.

Navarr said calmly: 'Miss Leonard, will you search the two women.'

'The women!' Rex ejaculated angrily.

'Why the women? Why the hell don't ya search her too while you're at it?'

Navarr ignored him while Kay rather tentatively ran her hands over Lorretta, and then Ruth Ballard. The actress seemed too stunned to argue, while the elderly woman still showed no interest in her surroundings. There was still no knife.

'All right,' Navarr said at last. 'So he was smarter than I am, he didn't risk retrieving the knife. But the fact still remains that one of us is a killer.'

Dorapho eyed him doubtfully. 'Are you sure of all this? Why would anyone want to kill the two flyers? Or Mr. Asaka? Or yourself?'

Navarr glanced down at the wicked bamboo arrow in his hands, then looked up again. 'I've been giving it some thought. I think that somebody here doesn't want Larrieux's report to get through. I think he's out to kill us all. Somebody here wants Nakai to be blasted to hell. One of us is working for Voron.'

Rex looked genuinely amused. 'That's

crazy! Why the hell should anyone here be working for Voron?'

'I think that's obvious. When we were shot down Larrieux believed that Voron had been bluffing when he had Calostro book that seat, bluffing to keep Larrieux from using the plane's radio in flight. But I don't think Voron *was* bluffing. He did have an agent to take that ticket from Calostro and board the plane. Perhaps he didn't hit on the idea of radioing for a fighter until afterwards, but I believe he had everything planned in advance. The agent was to kill Larrieux if he attempted to use the plane's radio, not knowing that all the evidence was to be wiped out by the fighter anyway. Voron must have considered his man expendable. Only that agent didn't die. He survived with us. And now he's out to silence everybody who knows what Voron plans to do on Nakai.'

There was another brooding silence. Then Lorretta said nervously: 'But would he? I mean, would this man carry on working for Voron, knowing that Voron had been willing to have him sacrificed when the plane was shot down?'

Navarr shrugged. 'To me Voron sounds a pretty ruthless swine. If we get out and ruin his plans and he then discovers that his agent survived with us I wouldn't give much for that man's chances. Failure in the communist world isn't exactly approved, in fact, it isn't even tolerated. I think Voron would have his own agent hunted down and executed if he knew that that man had done nothing to prevent us escaping from the jungle to wreck his plans. His agent must know that too, that's why he intends to kill us all and then survive alone. It's the only way he can survive.'

Dorapho said slowly. 'That is *if* one of us is a communist agent. We have nothing but your word to support such a theory.'

'How else can you explain Connors's and Kelley's murder? How else do you explain Asaka's disappearance and the attempt on my life?'

Dorapho frowned. 'We only have your word that the airmen did not die by accident. Again it is only your word that someone shot at you in the jungle. And Mr. Asaka may yet return.'

Navarr said flatly: 'Why would I lie? And if Asaka is alive why didn't he hear and answer our shouts? No, my friend, Asaka is dead, murdered, by the same man who killed the two airmen.'

Kay Leonard said tightly: 'Are you sure, Mr. Navarr? Are you sure that — that Scott and Hatch were . . . ' She couldn't say the last word. A haunted look masked her anguished face, her hands were clenched, and her lips trembling.

'I'm sorry,' Navarr faltered clumsily. 'Sorry I had to tell you like that.' He stopped, not knowing what else to say.

Schelde, his round face blank and his glasses reflecting the firelight said slowly: 'What are we to do? If this man means to kill us all, what can we do?' His eyes darted from one face to another.

Chang Lee said calmly: 'I think Mr. Navarr is correct. Mr. Asaka would not lose himself in jungle. If he has not returned something has happen to him. And there is no reason for Mr. Navarr to lie. His explanation is logical.'

Lorretta echoed Schelde's words: 'What are we going to do?' Her voice was shrill.

Dorapho said harshly: 'First we will not panic. We will cook this bird we have caught, and eat. Then we will set double watches and tomorrow we will go on. Nobody will go into the jungle alone. If one of us is a murderer he must not get a second chance.'

They stared at him dumbly, unwilling to dismiss the subject but not knowing what to say. The Greek picked up the half-roast quail that the air hostess had been turning above the fire before she had left to join in the search for the missing Chinese. He began to turn it again.

Navarr said: 'Wait a minute, can any of you alibi each other?'

Dorapho looked up; shook his head. 'I was alone.'

Schelde said nervously: 'Me too, I saw no one.'

Rex sat down and pulled at the flashy tie that still hung slackly from his neck. 'We were all alone, we all went in different directions.'

Lorretta said: 'Kay and I kept together.' Her voice was less shrill but low.

Navarr could think of nothing else. Apart from the girls it could be any of them. He sat down and stared bitterly into the red heart of the fire. Unless the killer eventually panicked and gave himself away, there was no way of finding out who he was. Navarr felt frustrated and alone.

The quail was cooked, and Dorapho shared it out. Lorretta accepted her share and then moved around the fire to where Navarr sat on his own. He met her eyes curiously as she sat beside him, and wondered why she was seeking his company. Most of the time she avoided him.

She answered his gaze uncomfortably as she tucked her legs beneath her. Her deep blue eyes were hesitant beneath her dark lashes, and when she spoke her voice was low; a whisper that no one else could hear.

'Mr. Navarr, I think you're wrong. There doesn't have to be a communist agent amongst us at all.'

He was surprised, almost startled. He studied her face for a moment and then said: 'Go on.'

She murmured quietly: 'I was thinking of Mrs. Ballard. She's barely spoken a dozen words since the plane crashed, and those we've had to force out of her. The death of her husband has hit her hard, and it's just possible that she holds the aircrew responsible in some way. There's no telling what is going on in her mind She may have killed Kelley and Connors out of some misdirected idea of vengeance. She may believe that they might have saved her husband if they had tried harder.'

Navarr said equally softly: 'It's possible, I suppose, and it would explain why the two airmen were killed. Only it doesn't explain Asaka's disappearance, or the arrow that was fired at me. We're not crew members.'

'No. But once a person with a twisted mind starts to kill they often go on, unable to stop.'

Navarr glanced across the clearing to where Ruth Ballard sat alone. He studied the elderly Englishwoman carefully, noticing the frail body, her silvering hair and the plump haggard face shadowed by rimless spectacles. He shook his head slowly.

'No, Lorretta, she couldn't do it. She might have managed Kelley and Connors, they were helpless and a child could have taken that swipe at Connors's fingers with a knife. She might possibly have fired that arrow at me. But it's too much to believe that she found a simple way of killing Asaka without him putting up a struggle. Perfect opportunities for murder with the victim helpless just don't happen that often.

'Asaka made no cry remember. We heard nothing. Whatever happened to him happened quickly, before he could do anything about it. That's what makes me sure he was killed by a trained agent. Asaka had no reason to fear any of us, he couldn't have suspected what his murderer intended, and by the time he did realise it, it was too late. A trained man could use a quick throat chop or a sudden stranglehold in a split second. That's the way I think it must have happened.'

Lorretta stared into the fire, her hands resting on her knees. The glow of the flames reflected in the shoulder-length wave of her golden hair, dancing in burning spangles of flickering light. Her face was slightly shiny from lack of make-up, but her lips were still red and as impishly kissable as ever. She finally looked back at Navarr and said slowly: 'I suppose you're right.' Her tone hardened a little then. 'I'll bet you're always right. It was just an idea.'

'What made you bring it to me?' He was genuinely curious.

She didn't answer for a moment and then she said: 'I don't like you, I suppose you've guessed that. You're too smart, too full of conceit, and after the other night I think you're a louse as well. But I don't think you're a murderer. That's why I thought you were the man to tell.'

Navarr grinned. 'Thanks for the little bit of faith anyway. And at least I can say the same for you. I don't think you killed them either.'

She knew he was laughing at her, but she didn't know it was his only defence against her scathing tongue. She got up and said acidly: 'Good-night.'

She walked back to the other side of the fire, her meal still uneaten in her hand. She sat down and began to tear at the half-cold leg of quail with angry teeth.

Schelde was beside her. He said abruptly: 'Do you think we will ever get out of this jungle, Miss Valoise? Any of us?' He sounded as though he wanted someone to reassure him very badly.

Lorretta looked up. 'Navarr will get out,' her tone was almost bitter. 'He's the kind of hard, lean, bastard who could get out of anything. Maybe some of us will get out with him, and maybe we won't. But Navarr will get out.'

★ ★ ★

They got up with the sun the following morning and made another fruitless search for Asaka's body. At last they moved on, Dorapho leading the way, and looking positively villainous in four days' growth of beard.

They moved wearily through the long day. They were wild-looking, their clothes ragged, and their faces streaked with sweat. The terrain was a little more level now, the parallel ridges not quite so high and farther apart. The rolling jungle still rose high around them, but occasionally they would have to push their way through wide stretches of tall elephant-grass that waved above their heads. Once they had to circle a rugged gorge that gashed the flank of a ridge. Twice they had to descend into low ravines and climb out again up the steep craggy sides. The sun blazed down with eternal, forceful waves, the solid heat beating relentlessly on their backs. Their marches became shorter and the spells of rest longer. They almost had to carry Ruth Ballard along, helping her every foot of the way. Navarr wondered how long they could keep it up.

Navarr was leading during the late afternoon and the swift rushing sound ahead barely made an impression on his mind when he first heard it. He was half-doped by the heat and was hardly aware that the others still trailed behind him. They were descending a low ridge, clothed in clinging jungle, and it was several moments before the growing sound penetrated Navarr's brain. He moved ahead slowly, trying to identify the sound. Then abruptly the tangle ahead of him parted and he came out on to a marshy carpet of knee-high reeds. He stopped. Ahead of them lay a river; a fast, sullen barrier of water nearly thirty yards across.

The rest of the party blundered to a halt around him, staring almost in wonderment at the rushing waters that swirled in fast currents around jagged rocks that reared from the river bed, hissing and foaming, charging relentlessly on. The sound was a dull roaring now, coupled with snarls and splashes as the water slapped against the rocks. The spray flew high and the air was damp. Thick reeds and feathery white rushes flanked the banks.

Rex was the first to speak. He blurted

loudly: 'Water, we can fill up again. Hell, but have I got a thirst.' He stumbled forwards through the dark green reeds, his feet squelching in the marshy ground.

Dorapho said sharply: 'Be careful. The water is fast and dangerous.'

Rex ignored him, splashing knee-deep through water and reeds. He scooped up a handful of water and brought it to his lips.

'Don't,' Kay Leonard called shrilly. 'That's not pure stream water like the last lot. It's probably full of germs.'

Rex let the water run through his cupped hands, turning back slowly to face her.

She went on: 'That stream came from a spring somewhere, this is rainwater. We'll have to boil it. If you must have a drink finish what's in the bags, we can fill up here anyway.'

Rex came back slowly and they all drank deeply from what little water they had left. They still carried with them the flask casing that Navarr had found at the spot where the plane crashed, Kay had insisted that they carry it as a possible cooking utensil, and now she suggested that they use it to boil their water rather than take chances.

Dorapho agreed and then added: 'But first I think we should cross this river. We can camp on the far side and pause to stock up on water and game before we go on.'

Schelde rubbed his lightly stubbled chin and said: 'The river is fast, very fast. It will be dangerous to try and cross. It is very fast.'

Dorapho studied the swirling currents grimly. 'We must go downstream,' he said at last. 'We must search for a safer place to cross.'

They turned south along the river bank, the Greek leading as they waded through the knee-deep sea of reeds and rushes. A bamboo thicket barred their path and they had to detour round it into the jungle. They rejoined the river a hundred yards farther down and found it still fast and dangerous. For almost half a mile they followed the course of the grey, tumbling waters until finally they came to a spot where the river widened by another dozen yards. It was still fast but did not appear to be so deep.

Dorapho said: 'I think we can cross here. It looks shallow enough to walk over, and provided we form a chain and go hand in hand none of us should be swept away. We must go carefully but I think we can do it.'

Schelde said again: 'It is fast, very fast.'

Navarr studied the surface of the river and decided that the Greek was right. It was now almost forty yards to the far bank but it looked to be no more than shoulder-deep. He said flatly: 'I'll go first. I'm a strong swimmer, and if I step in a hole I'll probably stand a better chance than the rest of you.'

Nobody argued and he walked out into the swirling river. He moved out several yards, up to his thighs, and felt the fierce pressure of the current pulling at his legs. It was fast, and very treacherous. He took another few paces and felt it trying to jerk his feet from under him. He glanced back and said grimly: 'Mrs. Ballard had better come next, the rest of you link up behind her. If anyone slips, the chain concentrates on standing firm until he or she regains her footing. If I find we can't make it we'll turn back.'

There were murmurs of assent and then Navarr moved back to take Ruth Ballard's hand. He knew that she was going to prove the weak link in the chain and felt that she would be safer in his grasp.

Navarr moved out again, murmuring a word of encouragement to the elderly woman who held his hand. She smiled at him faintly, but said nothing. He moved towards midstream with very slow steps, knowing that she was having much more difficulty in anchoring her feet than he was. The water swirled up around his waist, but the current seemed no stronger. He began to hope that they were going to make it easily, and moved on.

The river surged around his chest a few yards farther out, the current was strong and plucking at his legs but he had no real difficulty in holding firm.

He kept going tentatively, matching his speed to that of the woman's next to him. Once she slipped, but he held her until she found her footing again. They reached midstream and the pressure of the water was fierce. It was up to Navarr's shoulders and the little woman's neck. Navarr held her with both hands, one hand in hers, the other round her shoulders and supporting her beneath her armpit. The rest of the chain was strung out behind them.

Navarr felt the ground begin to rise again, and smiled encouragingly at the little woman. They were going to make it. The current was fast and deadly, but the firm and determined chain was coming through strongly.

Then the killer, who was walking next to Dorapho, suddenly and viciously used one foot to kick the Greek's feet from under him. In the same moment he let go of the man's hand. The current whirled Dorapho off his feet, and the force of it tore him away from the other half of the chain.

In seconds the rest of the chain were

floundering in disorder, and Dorapho was yelling as the river carried him away.

He went under, sucked down by the current. He didn't come up.

10

The Old Cat

Terror reigned as the remaining members of the party fought to retain their footing in the foaming waters of the river. The chain broke up completely, and the situation changed from one of near safety to disaster. Navarr looked back as the Greek's yells echoed above the rush and swirl of the river. Dorapho was gone, and the rest were splashing and shouting in alarm. At any moment they could be swept off their feet and carried downstream where the river deepened and the current made it impossible to swim.

Navarr cursed, and then strode out towards the bank. The depth was lessening and he made another ten yards, dragging Ruth Ballard behind him until the depth dropped below his hips. He pulled the elderly woman past him and gave her a shove towards the safety of the bank. Hurriedly he turned to face the others.

They were split up all over the place. Rex was a few yards downstream, swimming desperately and nearly within reach of the bank. Schelde was wading in towards him, still up to his waist in water. Behind him Chang Lee was moving with cautious, sliding steps. The river was surging round his chest, but his feet were still firmly anchored. Beyond them Kay and Lorretta still stood together in midstream, bracing themselves against the savage force of the river as it thrust against their straining bodies. They were still hand in hand and leaning into the current to prevent themselves being forced downstream. The cold grey surface of the torrent was washing above their shoulders.

Navarr splashed past Schelde, fighting the fierce pressure around his legs. At any moment the girls might panic and attempt to move, then they would be plucked off their feet and carried away. Navarr yelled at them to stand firm and forced his way past Chang Lee. The river surged around his chest and he had to move more cautiously to keep his footing.

Slowly he inched through the fury of rushing water into the centre of the stream. He saw the girls staring at him, their hair bedraggled, their eyes wide and frightened. Broken waves sprayed up in their faces. Desperately Navarr reached out with one arm through the roaring wall of water and found Kay's wrist. His fingers closed like a steel clamp.

'Hang on!' he bellowed. 'Hang on and move slowly like before.'

He started to inch his way back towards higher ground, towing the two girls behind him. They made two yards, two hard fought yards, and then Lorretta slipped, the current whipped her feet from under her and flung her body downstream.

But Kay held her. Ever since the chain had snapped they had held together, and now their grip had become locked solid. Not even the river could break it.

Navarr half turned to face them, leaning back into the current to counteract the sudden drag of Lorretta's weight. He dug his heels in firmly and braced his legs. Lorretta was trailing downstream, Kay stretched between them. Grimly Navarr pulled them both in. He got a grip above Kay's elbow with his right hand and hauled them closer. He hooked his left arm around her waist and transferred her arm around his neck. He could reach her other wrist now and together they pulled Lorretta in. Navarr then let go abruptly and grabbed the actress by the arm. He hauled her in hand over hand until she regained her footing beside him. Then, with an arm around each of them, he started to move again towards the bank. His heart was pounding crazily, and despite the proximity of so much water his mouth was dry.

The level dropped around them as the ground grew higher, and then at last they were splashing out on to dry land. Navarr stood there for a moment, his chest heaving and his limbs trembling. He supported the streaming bodies of the two girls, one on each side, as he gazed around. Schelde was on his knees, gasping for breath. Chang Lee was staring at the river, his mouth agape. Rex was staggering along the bank towards them, streaming water. Unceremoniously Navarr dropped both girls on the ground. He said tensely:

'Where's Dorapho?'

Rex answered, his voice weak and breathless. 'He was swept away. It was he who lost his footing. The clumsy fool almost had us all drowned.'

Chang Lee added hoarsely: 'I see him carried down river. He go under. Then I not see him any more.'

Navarr turned to face the river, the grey, swirling, treacherous river that rushed and roared onwards without pause. He knew there was no hope for the Greek, but he said grimly: 'We'd better go downstream, he may have been washed ashore somewhere.'

'If he is he'll be dead.' Rex sat down heavily as he spoke. 'That current sucked him under.'

'We'll search.' Navarr's tone was sour.

Schelde manoeuvred himself into a sitting position, his short, plump body still shivering. 'We — we must search,' his lips were quivering. 'We must search, but first I must get my breath. But we must search.'

Navarr sat down wearily between the two girls. They both lay where he had dropped them. Kay sprawled on her stomach, her shoulders heaving as she sucked in her breath. Lorretta had rolled over on to her back, her blonde hair spreading in a muddy tangle around her head. Her thin blouse was plastered close around the swelling curves of her breasts, but for once she was not posing her figure. Her eyes were closed and she looked almost unconscious.

Navarr said wearily: 'We'll get our breath back, then move downstream.' He was thinking of the water bags as much as the Greek. Chang Lee had hung on to one of their bows and a handful of arrows, but both water bags had been swept away. Before they could move on they would have to find one of them. Mentally he cursed the clumsiness of the Greek who had so seriously endangered their position.

★ ★ ★

The killer among them felt an almost overpowering sense of relief. The sudden impulse to kick the Greek's feet from under him had provided results, but could easily have gone wrong. Although the river had not claimed as many victims as had been hoped for, at least Dorapho was gone and without the water bags he had carried they were now stranded in the jungle. It was a pity that Navarr had survived though. A great pity. Navarr was the only dangerous adversary here now, that was clear. If ever a showdown came it would be with Navarr.

★ ★ ★

However the unknown killer's plans had not matured quite as fruitfully as they seemed to have done at first. After a thorough search along the river bank the survivors did find one of their invaluable water bags. It was wedged securely among a jumble of rocks farther downstream and Navarr retrieved it with little difficulty.

Dorapho they never saw again.

By then it was late and the sun was setting beyond the river, throwing red and yellow reflections in the water. They made camp as it faded beyond the nearest ridge, and the water that comprised Nico Dorapho's swirling tomb became black and menacing as it rushed past. The moon came up slowly, casting a sinister grey light over the river. It outlined the thick jungle on the far bank in black silhouette, throwing vague and menacing shadows as it rode the starry seas of the heavens. Deep in the jungle the jackals howled at it, their cries wailing like a ghostly death chant in the night.

After a while Navarr got up to feed the fire and set the watches. He resented the necessity to take the lead, but he knew that there was now no one else capable of doing so. The others accepted his authority without comment. Even Rex had lost all desire to take charge of the party.

They all lay awake for a long time, almost fearful of going to sleep. After only five days in the jungle they had lost four of their most capable men, and the fact was no aid to relaxed sleeping. Navarr lay awake longer than most, grimly thinking. He had six people to lead out of this jungle hell. And he had to get them out in time to prevent the mass murder of practically the whole population of the Nakai islands. The realisation that those thousands of lives rested on his shoulders alone made him sweat.

For a moment he visualised the results if Voron should succeed in his murderous scheme. The great gleaming American bomber that carried the hidden package of destruction moving slowly down the broad runway. And far up the mountainside in their rocky hideout Kang and Calostro would be listening in to the control tower clearing it for take-off. As the conversation between pilot and tower crackled over the radio, one of the agents would be watching the airfield through binoculars. The moment the giant bomber lifted into the air the remote control firing button would be pressed and the atom blast would shake the very island.

The bomber and airfield would be incinerated in seconds, the surrounding buildings flattened by the blast, and the racing shock waves would vibrate through the earth. Nothing would be left but the rushing smoke mushroom that would surge upwards at fantastic speed, spreading its wings of death over shattered Nakai.

But that would only be the beginning. The repercussions of the blast would be felt in every corner of the earth. Enquiries would be held into the disaster, and the few survivors from Nakai would be able to tell only one thing: that an American bomber had been just clearing the ground when it disintegrated into a blinding flash-ball of orange fire. That one fact, together with the communist propaganda machine, would damn the U.S. Air Force in the eyes of the world. The only possible verdict from the enquiry would be that someone on Nakai air base had been careless, and the Air Force would be accused of criminal negligence. America's prestige in Asia, and in Africa too, would be destroyed, whole countries might turn to place their trust in communism overnight. The condemnation of the American Strategic Air Command, the shield of the free world, would be enough to sway the impressionable masses of Asia, Africa, and the Middle East into accepting the double-edged protection of the communist world. The damage would be irredeemable. The whole course of history could be turned on to a path of despair.

One of them had to survive to stop it. Despite the jungle and the killer in their midst, one of them *had* to survive.

Navarr's mind was still full of his terrible responsibility when he finally fell asleep. For the moment there was nothing he could do but relax until dawn, but even as he slept an expression of grim determination masked his features. His face, with its short, scrubby black beard, looked dark and terrible in the glow of the flickering flames.

★ ★ ★

The night passed, and deeper in the jungle a sinuous shape paused in its silent passage through the forest. A shaft of moonlight found its way through the black canopy of trees, lighting up with a pale glimmer the long tawny body. The old cat was lean; an ageing tiger with fiery eyes and gently swishing tail. He moved on through the dense tangles, lurching slightly as he walked for one paw was cruelly twisted. It was a forepaw, a paw that had been caught between the sharp edges of a narrow crevice in the rocks as he streaked after his prey many moons past. The cat had screamed as the bone broke and he had plunged down the slope of the rocky hillside. His prey had escaped, and he had lain up for days to rest and lick at his broken foot with a rasping tongue. At last hunger had driven him from his lair but hunting was a task that needed four swift legs. He couldn't reach any speed with three and a painful, twisted forepaw. So he had grown hungrier, his meals unsatisfying and infrequent. Tonight he was hungry again, dragging his empty belly through the undergrowth as he searched for game. From far away near the river bank he caught a new scent. He sniffed the air, wrinkling his nose and showing his teeth in a deep-throated growl. His eyes glowed in the blackness.

★ ★ ★

The moon was half hidden by a bank of cloud as Navarr took his turn at watch by the fire. His thoughts kept dissolving and he knew that he was nodding off to sleep. Determinedly he got up and moved about. He threw more wood on the fire and paused to listen to the noises of the night. The frogs were still croaking and the mosquitoes buzzed faintly. From somewhere in the jungle came a strange coughing grunt. Something big he decided and he built the fire higher.

When his watch was over he woke Chang Lee. The strange grunting sound lingered in his memory, and he warned the Chinese to keep the fire burning well before he allowed himself to relax into sleep.

★ ★ ★

The crippled cat lay on his belly, the strange new scent close in his slightly twitching nostrils. Some inherited instinct warned him that the source of the new scent could be dangerous. But he needed blood-fresh meat. He had to eat or starve. He slunk nearer to the firelight.

For a long time he lay low on his belly and waited. Waited for the fire to grow dim. The fierce, burning eyes had already selected a victim; a still form that lay silent in sleep. The old cat began to inch closer as the circle of firelight grew smaller.

At last he rose slowly, balancing on three paws. Then, like a snarling, tawny streak of destruction, he erupted into a clumsy charge, leaping desperately into the frightening glimmer of the fire.

11

Stalked

Navarr awoke to a shrieking scream from Lorretta as the crippled cat landed in the camp. The sound electrified him and brought him springing to his feet. For a moment he stood motionless as the scene registered itself in his sleep-numbed brain. Their fire was almost dead and in the vague light it threw he saw the tawny, shadowy form of the tiger. For a second he didn't even recognise it and then the old cat let out a snarling roar, its teeth gleamed and the eyes flashed like fiery emeralds. It had landed astride Kay Leonard and she was screaming with pain and fear. Panic reigned as the rest of the party scattered amid yells of terror and confusion. Someone kicked through the fire and spread burning brands about the camp-site.

The big cat roared again and tossed its

great head in defiance. Then the great jaws clamped shut on Kay's shoulder and he lurched back into the jungle, dragging her screaming through the undergrowth.

The few seconds that Navarr had taken to appreciate the situation were almost fatal. The tiger and his victim were already disappearing from view when Navarr snatched up a flaming brand from the fire and raced forward. The cat bellowed with rage as the mass of orange flame lunged into his savage face. The fierce heat singed the side of the massive neck as he jerked his head aside. Desperately Navarr jabbed again, grabbing Kay by the arm at the same time. The cat backed frantically through the jungle, dragging them both and tossing his great head to avoid the flaming brand. Then, abruptly, he released his hold on the screaming girl, wheeled around, and bolted in his crazy lurching run back into the jungle.

Navarr had finished up on his knees beside the still body of Kay Leonard, and he struggled hurriedly to his feet. He could hear the fast disappearing tiger crashing through the jungle night and he hurled his fiery torch savagely in the same direction. It was a futile gesture that had all his strength behind it. The twisting torch arched through the night, struck a curtain of vines and then landed sizzling in a bed of wet bracken.

Navarr turned to Kay and picked her up carefully. He could barely see her in the darkness but he could feel her blood on his hands where he held her. He was unsure whether she was alive or dead, and he stumbled hurriedly back to the faint glimmer that remained of their fire. The undergrowth caught at his feet and branches whipped his face. Kay was a dead weight in his arms.

The others were standing in a bunch directly behind the scattered fire; their faces pale and shaken. Lorretta broke away from them and went towards Navarr, her face was suddenly bloodless and she shut her eyes and looked away when she saw Kay.

Navarr said harshly: 'Rebuild that fire. Move!'

The three men looked startled and

then hurriedly began to kick the fire together and throw more wood on the flames. Within a minute or two they had a reasonable blaze again.

Navarr laid the air hostess close to the fire where he had the best light. A feeling of horror shuddered through him when he saw her clearly and he knew how the actress had felt. The girl had been savaged terribly by the old cat. Her jacket had been torn away, and her right shoulder was soaked with blood, her blouse lay open, and one white breast had been raked by the razor-edged claws. Her left thigh had been cruelly mauled. She was alive, but only just.

'Let me come.'

Navarr looked up to see Lorretta kneeling beside him. Her face was white, and her lips were compressed together. 'We need bandages,' she said, 'something to staunch the blood.' Her hands touched her silken blouse then came away. 'It's yellow,' she said. 'The dye might poison her.'

Navarr pulled off his jacket and then tore off his shirt. 'It's sweaty, none too clean,' he said doubtfully.

Lorretta took it. 'It's better than the dye,' she said. She clenched her teeth and began to clean the blood away from the unconscious girl's shoulder. Navarr pulled out his knife and flicked open the blade, carefully he cut away the blood-soaked blouse and bra. When he had finished he looked up.

'More shirts,' he said tightly. 'Strip them off.'

The three men obeyed, handing over their shirts for bandages and then putting back their jackets. Schelde was holding Ruth Ballard who was crying against his shoulder. Rex was looking frightened and angry. The Chinese, who had let the fire almost out, began guiltily to heap more wood on to the blaze.

Lorretta did her best to check the blood that still flowed from Kay's shoulder and breast, while Navarr used the knife to slit one of the shirts into strips. When he had finished he supported the air hostess while Lorretta bound a thick pad about the savaged shoulder. Lorretta's face was still chalk-white and her lips never moved;

even so her hands were sure and gentle. Navarr was beginning to feel sick.

When the shoulder was bandaged they turned their attention to the mauled thigh. Again Navarr used the knife to cut away the blue skirt and what was left of the silk stocking, the lacerations in the white flesh were long and deep. Lorretta cleaned and bandaged them as best she could. Afterwards they managed to bind a clumsy pad about the ugly, but less serious wounds across the white breast. It was an awkward job, for Kay's erratic breathing was disturbing the bandage all the while, but finally they got it fixed. Navarr made the injured girl more comfortable by pillowing her head with his jacket. Lorretta used the top half of her costume to cover her up.

At last they stood up slowly.

Chang Lee said nervously: 'Will Miss Kay be alive?'

Navarr wiped the sweat from his face, his bare chest was glistening in the firelight. He said tightly: 'I don't think so. If we could get her to a hospital they might save her, but out here — '

His words trailed off, and he gestured helplessly with his hands.

'She has lost a lot of blood, she is very bad.' Schelde shook his head sadly, and then with his irritating habit of stressing emphasis by repetition added: 'She has lost too much blood.'

Rex said fiercely: 'Who was on watch?' He had taken off his flashy tie when he stripped off his shirt and now he was twisting it angrily between his fingers. The sweat was trickling down from his receding hair line. 'Who let that Goddamned fire out?'

Chang Lee refused to meet the American's eyes. He said miserably: 'I am to blame. I almost go back to sleep.'

Fear was the basis of Rex's anger, he clamped a big hand on the lapel of the Chinese's jacket and snapped viciously: 'Goddamn it, I oughta take you apart. You near enough killed that poor kid. That cat would never have come near us if you'd kept the fire high.'

'Please, I am sorry.'

'Gentlemen!' Schelde said in alarm. He laid a tentative hand on Rex's arm. 'Gentlemen, please?'

'Sorry!' Rex was sneering. 'I guess it's a bit too late to be sorry. How sorry do you think she's feeling?'

Navarr said evenly: 'Ease up, Rex. Ease up.'

'To hell with easing up! This guy coulda got the lot of us killed.'

The Chinese was still trying to pull away. He was making no real attempt to defend himself, but his hands seemed ready and his slitted eyes were wary. He said again: 'I am sorry. I am asleep on watch. Through me Miss Kay is hurt. I am not happy. This does not make me feel good.' His mis-phrased English came in short staccato sentences, edged with tension.

'So you are not happy,' repeated Rex. 'You are not feeling good.' He shook off Schelde's nervously retaining hand without sparing the little man a glance. 'You Goddamned Chink, you're gonna be so unhappy that you'll never feel good again.'

'Mr. Rex, we are foolish. It is not good to fight — '

'You're right, buddy, for you it ain't. I'm gonna — '

Navarr closed his right hand around the American's wrist, his left on Chang Lee's jacket. With a wrench he tore them apart. He pushed both men away and snapped: 'When I said ease up I meant it.'

Rex had gone almost too far to retreat. He blustered angrily: 'Who the hell are you to — '

Lorretta stepped suddenly forwards and slapped the American hard about the face.

'Now shut up,' she burst out angrily. She spun to face the others. 'Shut up all of you! Kay is dying, and all you can do is fight like a lot of stupid kids. Just shut up and keep quiet.' She glared from one to the other and her palm was open, ready to slap down the next man who spoke.

No one did, even Rex was shamed into silence.

Lorretta hesitated as they fell silent, then she turned away in a quick, sharp movement and knelt again by the limp figure of Kay Leonard. The dark girl was still breathing, but her face was a greyish pallor and beaded with sweat. Her slim body stirred painfully and her head twisted from side to side. In her coma, she moaned repeatedly through bloodless lips.

The four men watched silently as the actress cushioned Kay's head in her lap and used a scrap of cloth from one of the shirts to wipe the perspiration from the damp temples. There was nothing they could do for the air hostess, and after a few minutes Schelde moved closer to the still weeping Ruth Ballard and made the little Englishwoman sit down. Rex and the Chinese still glared at each other, Rex still twisting and tugging at his tie. Navarr felt helpless, and more alone than ever before in his lonely existence. The sense of personal failure within him almost equalled that of his grief for the dying girl. He had heard what he now realised was the coughing grunt of the tiger while on watch, he should have foreseen this. In his own way he felt almost as guilty as the hapless Chinese.

For the rest of the night Lorretta supported Kay's head on her lap, but her vigil was a hopeless one. Just before dawn Kay Leonard died. Her last words were the whispered names Hatch and Scott, both uttered in almost the same breath. She had never fully recovered consciousness.

They buried her deep in the soft soil and covered the grave with the largest boulders they could find to foil the scavengers of the jungle.

The brief burial service left them grim-faced but dry-eyed, for violent death held no shock for them by now. Even Lorretta stayed her tears. She was no longer the blonde bombshell of the screen. The jungle had hardened her, and now she made no more scenes. Ruth Ballard, as always, seemed unaware of what was taking place around her.

After the burial they moved on, staying only long enough to boil up the water to fill their single bag. While they waited, Navarr and Rex managed to shoot a brace of pheasants and a turkey which they carried with them. They were finding their weapons quite serviceable, and were both becoming fair shots. It was while he was hunting that Navarr found the tracks of the old tiger and followed them a few yards into the jungle. The earth was soft and the paw marks were clear, one paw had a curiously twisted mark, the claws turned inwards and the heel of the pad sinking deep on one edge. Navarr recalled the animal's lurching run and realised that the cat was crippled. He guessed that it was too slow to catch its normal game and shivered at the possible results of its having now tasted human blood. He was glad to rejoin his companions and find them ready to go.

They were nearly a mile away from the river when Navarr made the infuriating discovery that they had left their single bow and arrows behind. He swore futilely. Somebody had to go back for them and he was the fittest man in the party. Telling the others to wait he retraced his steps, taking nearly an hour to get back to their camp-site by the river.

It was then that he saw the pawprints.

They were all around the dead fire, plain deep pad marks, and among them the curiously twisted print of the broken paw. Navarr felt a band of fear tightening around his chest. He wondered where the brute was now.

He drew Larrieux's automatic and kept it in his hand as he gathered up the bow and arrows. Swiftly he hurried back. He kept the gun ready and tried to convince himself that the report would scare the cat away if it appeared.

There was something eerie about the jungle now that he had to travel it alone, something sinister about every shadow. Normally Navarr preferred his own company, but now he would be glad to rejoin his companions.

He had nearly come up with them when he had to cross a small clearing in the undergrowth. The soil was soft and sandy here, and smack in the middle of it was a clear print of the large twisted paw.

Navarr stared into the tangle of foliage and fern about him. The sweat was trickling down his back, and almost without realising it he flipped back the safety catch on the puny-calibred automatic.

He hurried on, certain now that the crippled cat was stalking them, waiting his chance to seize this new and slow-moving prey that had invaded his jungle home.

12

Live Bait for a Tiger

That night they built a roaring fire to keep the prowling cat at bay, but despite that they still found the twisted pawprints around their camp the next morning. It was clear that the cat had circled them several times, searching for some way to snatch a victim without coming in range of the fire. After Navarr had thrust the fiery torch in his face he had found a new respect for the fire.

Hurriedly they moved on, keeping in a close bunch with Navarr leading the way. Rex came next with the water bag, Chang Lee behind him with the bow and the two remaining birds. Schelde and Lorretta helped Ruth Ballard at the rear. It was an order that never varied now.

They made good time. By noon they had covered something like six miles, the best ever. None of them wanted to linger in the same region as the crippled cat. When Navarr finally called a halt they were feeling utterly exhausted, and collapsed gratefully on a clear stretch of hillside.

As he rested Navarr found himself thinking of his other problem: the identity of the murderer among them. He had been keeping a close watch on his companions, but none of them gave him any cause for suspicion. So he had to suspect them all.

He kept hoping that Dorapho had been the communist agent, because Dorapho was dead and they would no longer be in any danger. But somehow he knew it was not going to be as easy as that. Something that might have been intuition told him that the killer was still with them. It had to be one of the three men: Rex, who lay flat on his back, his hat pulled down over his face; Chang Lee who sat with his arms folded on his knees, staring through narrow eyes into the dense jungle at the foot of the hillside; or dumpy little Wilhem Schelde who tried so hard to instil Ruth Ballard with some interest in life, only to fail completely. It had to be one of them.

He began to wonder how the killer would decide to strike him down, for he knew that he must certainly be the next man on the agent's list. He was the only one left now who was capable of getting them all out alive. There was no false modesty in Navarr, and he rated himself as confident rather than conceited. Navarr could accept facts without undue emotion, and he began to wonder when the killer would make his attempt. Or would he wait in the hope that the stalking cat would do it for him?

★ ★ ★

The mind of the killer was assessing the same kind of thoughts. It was an almost unbelievable stroke of luck that the crippled tiger had appeared to take on the task of killing off the remaining survivors, but it was a pity that the air hostess had to be the first to die in such a horrible manner. The agent still felt bad about that. Kay had been a pleasant and likeable young woman, who had done nothing to deserve such a grim death.

In actual fact the agent felt sick with all the deaths that had occurred. The murder of a stranger you had never seen until the moment of killing was one thing; it could be paralleled with wartime methods when thousands killed to order in action. But the deliberate elimination of people who trusted you was something different. These people you knew as friends and although they were enemies their murder became a particularly loathesome crime.

But what choice was there? When your friends and family could be made to suffer the punishment of your failure, what choice did you have? The answer was simple: when you worked under a cold, calculating machine like Voron there was no choice at all. Voron had neither pity nor toleration for agents who failed.

The agent began to hope then that the cat would attack Navarr. Without the tall cynic the rest would soon die in the jungle. There would be no need for further killing then, the agent could slip away alone. If only the cat would attack Navarr!

* * *

A few miles behind them the lean-flanked terror of their imaginations stood above a steep precipice that earlier had caused them to detour. The sunlight shone on his sleek black-orange coat, and reflected like bursts of flame from the savage eyes. The cat stood on three paws, tail swishing slowly, the twisted foot held up from the ground. His belly rumbled emptily and there was still the taste of blood on his snarling jaws. The stiff bristles around the flared nostrils twitched angrily as he stared down the steep drop to the thick jungle that had swallowed up his quarry.

He didn't want to go down there. It was strange ground, different from his own domain where he knew every branch and every tree; where every gorge, hillside and ravine were etched clearly in his mind. He didn't like unknown territory, he was wary of it, half afraid. But he was also hungry, ravenously hungry. He had tasted blood for the first time in days, and he knew that the slow-moving forms he had trailed would be easy to catch. His chance must come.

He snarled, rage trembling in his deep throat. Then abruptly a decision was formed in his savage mind. He turned and slunk swiftly through the jungle, following the scent trail that would lead him down the precipice where his quarry had gone.

★ ★ ★

Ahead Navarr was again leading the small party of survivors towards the east. The sweat was drenching his body as it always did, whether on the move or lying still. The other five were in their same order behind him and he could hear them crashing and stumbling in his wake. They had descended the other side of the hill where they had rested and were now pushing through a small plain of high, yellowing elephant-grass. The grass rose several feet above their heads, and snapped and crunched as he kicked a path through it. The grass-tops waved and danced in the disturbance of their passage. Navarr found the going easier than the jungle, but he was far from feeling at ease; this was perfect attacking country for the crippled tiger if he was still on their trail.

The elephant-grass ended at last and Navarr heaved a sigh of relief as they started up the slope of yet another jungle-flanked ridge. The sun was high and the humid air was sticking like vaporous glue to their lungs. They were moving in the eternal state of sweat and weariness that never left them in the jungle.

An hour or so later they had descended the ridge and started across the valley beyond. Navarr was still in the lead, concentrating his thoughts and energy on forcing a path through the massed barrier ahead of him. He didn't realise that his companions were beginning to straggle.

Chang Lee had been blundering along behind Rex for a long time, his wavering gaze fixed on the lurching shoulders of the man in front. Time after time he clawed off his hat and mopped his face and temples with the wet, floppy cloth, but still the moisture bubbled endlessly from his skin. He was feeling weak and dizzy, and when the distance between himself and the American's broad back began to grow wider he was past caring. He stumbled on and then the long bow he carried caught in a tangle of roots near his feet and he tripped over it, crushing the vegetation as he fell.

He lay there in a daze, breathing in the sweetish smell of the sap that oozed from the broken branches, and with it the tangy smell of his own sweat. The beating sun seemed to be trying to hammer him into the earth with pounding blows of solid heat.

Schelde and the two women almost walked past him before they pulled to a halt, all three of them nearly collapsing with the effort of breaking from the set pattern of their movements. Schelde stooped and got his hand under Chang's arm. He heaved but there was no strength left in his body. He had to stop and gasp for breath.

Chang felt the hand pulling him and made a determined effort to get up. He reached his knees slowly and then, with the little man's help he staggered upright. He said, 'thank you,' the two words slurring in his dry throat. Schelde smiled, a dull smile with the sweat laying like a tracery of beaded canals along the creases. His glasses looked misty and the Chinese wondered if he could see at all.

Schelde started to move after Rex and Navarr, dragging the two women with him. It was a few moments before they could get into stride again and they lurched like a trio of drunks after a beano. Chang Lee watched them stupidly and then fell in behind them. He knew they shouldn't be strung out like this. The tiger might still be stalking them. But he hadn't the energy to catch up and close up the gaps. He hadn't the energy to call out to the two in front to slow up either. He found his fumbling stride again and followed on in the rear.

The long bow snagged once or twice

as he struggled on, and he began to hate the clumsy awkwardness of the weapon. He was tempted to throw it away, but he didn't. Without it they would be unable to hunt. They would starve. Besides, Navarr would probably turn on him in a cold unemotional rage if he did. It was crazy to think of a man getting angry without emotion, but that was the way it would be with the Englishman. Chang was almost as frightened of Navarr as he was of starving without the bow. The sun was unbearable, and he began to wonder whether it was possible for a man to drown in his own sweat.

* * *

Half-way across the valley the crippled cat lay in wait. For the last half hour he had never been more than a few hundred yards away from the small group of survivors and now he had circled ahead. The walls of his empty stomach were aching painfully and he was feeling weak. His instinct told him that his days were numbered; had been ever since the crack in the rocks had broken his forepaw. But he was not ready to die, not while he had found this easily caught quarry to hunt. And now, now that they had no flames to defend them, they should prove easy prey.

The twisted paw was stretched in front of him as he waited, and the eternal nagging pain made him smooth his great tongue over it in slow rasping movements. His ears were alert, and the fierce eyes burned in the direction of the approaching men.

He saw Navarr push past within twenty feet of where he lay and an unspoken snarl vibrated in his throat. He recognised the man as his enemy, the man who had thrust fire in his face. His eyes blazed with hatred but his caution was stronger than his hate. He let Navarr go past. He watched the second man stumble by, but the others were too close. The old cat was wary of this new game when it kept so close together. He let Schelde and the girls pass, too, and then his fiery gaze fixed on the straggling Chinese.

He watched every move as Chang Lee

lurched past in the wake of the rest, then a low, almost silent, growl issued from his throat. Belly-low, the big cat began to close in, his tail swished slightly and the white jaws glinted in the sun.

Navarr heard Chang Lee's frantic scream as the crippled cat suddenly erupted out of the low vegetation to the left of their trail. Like a streak of tawny fire it leapt high into the air, the savage impact of its spring sending Chang sprawling to the earth. Navarr whirled and instinctively fumbled for the gun in his waistband. Through a haze of sweat he saw the Chinese writhing beneath the tawny shape of the cat, their bodies mixed together in a squirming tangle and the screams of the man rising above the snarling roars of the beast. Navarr lurched forwards at a run, firing his puny automatic into the air as he knocked Rex aside. He crashed past Schelde and the women, firing desperately as the cat turned and bolted, the Chinese still in its jaws. In desperation Navarr fired two more shots straight at the cat and saw it jerk its massive head and roar in its throat as the bullets stung its lean flank. Then it vanished into the low curtain of jungle, carrying the screaming Chang Lee with it. The crashing sounds of its retreat faded, and the screams of the Chinese died with them.

There was nothing that they could do. Nothing at all. Grimly Navarr led them on, his face a black, rugged mask of determined rage. Despite all his efforts he had lost another man, and for a moment despair made him believe that fate must surely have decreed that they should all die. Then defiance hardened within him. One of them would survive. *He* would survive. Despite the heat, the jungle, the stalking cat, and the killer among them, *he* would survive. And with him any of them that could stick the pace.

The next two days were like all the others since their peaceful airliner had been murderously shot out of the sky. They walked, rested, walked, and walked again, forcing their way ever eastwards across the endless jungle-flanked hills of Burma, crossing eternal ridges and valleys, descending or circling slashing ravines and gorges, or slithering down endless boulder-strewn slopes. They pushed wearily through the tenacious barrier of tangled vines and dense foliage, stumbled over roots and shrubs and sweated in the merciless heat of the sun. Like stumbling puppets they fought their way on, driven into a crazed frustration by the never-ending greenery of fern and bamboo, and the constant choking tangle of vegetation.

On the third night after Chang's death they camped in a low ravine. All were badly showing signs of the ravaging effect the jungle was having on them, and Navarr began to wonder how long it would be before they collapsed from malnutrition. The small amounts of food and water that he allowed them were nowhere near enough to support them through their ordeal, but strict rationing was a necessity. Most surprising of all was Ruth Ballard, who with Schelde's constant support was sticking the pace well. Schelde seemed to regard her as his personal responsibility ever since he had pulled her out of the burning plane.

After a while, Navarr moved away from the fire and stood alone, watching the stars glitter like strewn jewels through the awning of branches above. The moon was high and bright in the sky, and the dim luminosity that filtered down was barely enough to outline his lean features.

A voice said softly: 'Steve.'

He turned in surprise. Lorretta was standing beside him, a dark silhouette in the faint moonlight. It was the first time that she had ever used his Christian name, and he wondered where she had got it from. He didn't ask, merely decided that she must have heard it from Kay Leonard who would have known from the passenger list. He said simply: 'Hello.' His expression didn't change and his black-bearded face looked fearsome in the sudden flare of light from the fire.

She said quietly: 'Do you mind — my calling you Steve, I mean?' She hesitated. 'Kay told me.'

He grinned, his teeth showing extra white in the blackness of his face. 'Not at all, it's probably much more friendly than some of the things you must have been calling me lately.'

Her blue eyes were angry. 'Still the comedian — that same old cynical comedian — if you had a good friend he might do you the favour of telling you that nobody here thinks you're funny, except perhaps yourself.'

'Didn't I offer to be good friends with you once?' He just couldn't resist the insulting comeback, it was too good to pass up.

She looked away angrily, and for a moment he thought she was going to return to the fire. She didn't. She stared at the dozing forms of their three companions and then said suddenly: 'What are our chances, Steve? Of getting out I mean?'

'Fifty-fifty, maybe less.'

She looked back at him. 'You really think they're that high? With that cat still about, and the possibility that one of those three is a communist agent out to make sure that we don't survive?'

Navarr folded his arms across his chest, feeling the cloth of his jacket scratch harshly at his skin. 'It depends on our luck,' he told her. 'The cat got away with a meal. It'll lay up for a day or two, and we're already two days' travel away from his territory. I don't think we'll see him again. And as for the killer, it might have been Dorapho or Chang Lee. I'm hoping that it was.'

She looked doubtful. 'I don't know, I don't think it was either of them.'

'Then who do you think it is?'

Her shoulders shrugged. 'I don't know. I keep thinking, and watching them. But I just don't know. I don't think any of them could be a murderer, but — '

'So you've sacked your intuition, you don't even suspect Ruth Ballard any more?'

Her eyes angered at the trace of sarcasm in his voice. She said flatly: 'No. Ruth couldn't do it.'

He smiled, but said nothing.

She moved a step closer and asked abruptly: 'What makes you so sour, Steve?' She smiled quickly. 'You know, I used to live an act once, always making scenes, annoying people, acting the big screen star. I had to drop it out here though, it just didn't get me anywhere.' The smile flickered back. 'I've been wondering how long you'll keep up your act, Steve; the tough, lonewolf act. You really enjoy it don't you?'

Navarr grinned. 'Maybe it isn't an act.'

'I amuse you don't I?' She realised it without annoyance. 'Why?'

The expression on her face held his gaze. Humour danced in the blue depths of her eyes, the corners of her mouth lifted up in a half smile. Her hands were playing unconcernedly with the leaves of a small bush that grew level with her slim waist. He realised abruptly that she in her turn was amused by him. He said sharply, hurtfully: 'Some things are funny.' And then regretted it instantly.

She stopped playing with the leaves, her hands lingering in mid-movement. She said slowly: 'You really don't give a damn for anybody do you? Perhaps that's why no one has ever given a damn for you.'

'What gives you that idea, that no one has ever given a damn for me?'

'It has to be that way, it's the only thing that would drive a man into that cynical shell.'

He laughed, a slightly forced laugh that had an unnatural sound. 'So you're a psychologist too, analysing all my emotions and actions. I suppose the fact that I once parted my hair on the right means that I hate my father? Or the length of my nose makes me a kleptomaniac?' He paused. 'Who's couch did you learn on?'

She began to play with the leaves again. When she looked up her face was full of shadows in the dim moonlight.

'What have you got against me Steve? I didn't make much of an impression when we first met, I know. In fact, afterwards I even felt a sneaking sense of admiration for the way you stood your ground in that doorway. It did me good to have to walk round a man instead of having him jump aside. But why keep sneering at me now? The jungle's changed me — for the better I think. Why do you have to keep up your act?'

She left the leaves and their faces were

suddenly very close as she repeated: 'What have you got against me Steve?'

Navarr felt vaguely uncomfortable at the way the conversation was going. He found himself wishing that he had never started it. He wondered what he did really have against her. He wasn't really sure and he was aware of those penetrating blue eyes watching him closely, filled with hidden amusement. He said at last: 'I guess you might call it jealousy, a kind of natural resentment for someone who's really got it easy, or had it easy.'

She stared at him. Then a smile broke over her face and she shook with silent laughter. She chuckled and turned away, her shoulders still shaking. He stared at her dumbly and wondered what the hell he had said that was so funny.

She turned back at last, straight-faced but with her eyes still dancing. 'And I suppose you've had to go it alone?' she declared solemnly. 'You've never been spoilt or pampered, or in a position to throw a tantrum when you felt like it. You've always been the tough, lone wolf.'

Despite the mocking solemnity, her tone was taunting. It made Navarr feel he ought to writhe beneath it. He was already hazy on how this unwanted conversation had started, but he couldn't back out now. He found a smile and said casually: 'I've no complaints.'

'Like hell you haven't! You know, I've been wondering how dumb you are beneath that tough exterior. Well, now I know. Buddy, you ought to have a cupboard full of prizes for being dumb.'

Navarr gave her a sarcastic grin and remained silent, mostly because he had nothing to say.

She sobered suddenly.

'Do you think I was always Lorretta de Valoise, the big movie star?' Her mood had changed and her eyes were cold. 'Do you think I was born on the stage with a script in my hand? Surely not even you can be that dumb?'

She waited for an answer, but Navarr said nothing.

She went on: 'It takes a lot of hard work and a lot of lonely years to get where I got to. I was born plain little Sally

Jones in a plain little four-roomed house in Clapham. I was a plain runny-nosed kid for four years, and then a plain spotty-faced schoolgirl until I was fifteen. And even then I wasn't particularly beautiful.' She swept both hands up suddenly and pushed her hair back behind the nape of her neck. 'Take a close look at my face, mister! The cheeks are a bit too thin to be really beautiful, that's why I grow my hair long and sweep it round the front to frame my face and hide the leanness. I suppose that makes me a cheat in your book? It isn't even blonde either. If you look close at the roots after seven days you'll see it's a dull auburn instead.' Her tone was hard, almost brittle now. 'Maybe they told you sometime that the stage was an overcrowded profession. Well that isn't half of it. It's nothing but a bloody rat race. It took me seven long years to reach the top, and if I wasn't going it alone in those seven years then I don't ever want to know what being alone is like.'

She paused for breath. 'Do you know what it's like? Tramping around agencies. Going hungry. Getting bit parts. Tramping the agencies again. Having fat, bald men telling you they can help you if only you'll be nice. I stuck that for seven years before I made the grade. And now I'm near the top. Not at the top but near enough, near enough to be able to make life hell for some of those fat, bald men. I figure I have a right to get my own back. I figure I had a right to act the way I did. I had to work my way up there for seven lonely, stinking years.'

She stopped, her face still set hard. Her lips clamped shut and suddenly she turned away. She stood with her back to him, wondering why she had to pour out her life story to the tall, sarcastic character behind her. She didn't even like him. Her shoulders were trembling slightly.

Navarr said slowly: 'Was Barney one of those fat, bald men?' He felt he had to say something.

It was several minutes before she turned round, by then the words seemed to have softened her anger. She shook her head and answered: 'No, Barney was different. Barney was really in love with me. And

I played on it. Nobody else could have played Barney up like I did. When the plane crashed I was too frightened to fasten my safety belt. Barney did it for me but never had time to fix his own. I felt such a louse. All that time I'd been taking it out on the wrong man.' Her eyes were wet, and for a moment he thought she was going to cry.

Minutes passed, minutes in which they stood together yet each strangely alone just beyond the range of the firelight. Their three companions were asleep and the fire still danced high. Above them the sky sparkled in starry beauty through the tracery of branches. The sounds of the jungle seemed very vague and distant, as if filtering through from another world.

Then Navarr said suddenly: 'You're right, I am dumb.'

She looked up as he straightened away from his supporting tree. Her eyes were uncertain and her lips trembled with the movement of barely checked words. The moonlight made a pale silver glory of her hair, but he wouldn't have cared if it had been dull auburn. His big hands reached out and held her gently by the waist. He drew her towards him and this time there was no resistance.

Their lips closed in a tender, half-fearing kiss. He felt the lift of her breasts, the tips pressing through the thin silk blouse and touching his bare chest. Then her arms locked around his shoulders, and they came together slowly, their bodies closing like the walls of a vice. They clung together fiercely, brutally. Navarr's hand rose to cup the back of her head, feeling the soft hair flow over his hand as he held her mouth to his lips. She strained against him, desiring, demanding. Her eyes were closed, but her yearning body seemed a part of his own.

Somewhere in the jungle an unheeded jackal howled to the moon.

* * *

At dawn the next morning Rex went out hunting. He returned with two plump birds and grim news. There were more pawprints around their camp, the peculiar twisted prints of the crippled cat. It had been circling their camp during the night.

Lorretta said slowly: 'I thought we were out of his territory. I thought we'd left him behind.'

Navarr's face was a black, unshaven mask. 'We are out of his territory. He must be pretty ravenous to stalk us this far, and I guess that we must now be the only game that he can hunt.'

Rex stared at the pawprints, the twisted symbols of lurking death.

'What can we do?' he asked tightly. 'We've got to keep moving, so it's pretty certain that he'll get another one of us.'

Navarr hesitated, then he answered: 'We can kill him first.'

Rex looked up, his fair, bearded face suddenly haggard. 'How?' he demanded. 'With that stupid gun? Or a bow and arrow?'

Schelde said unhappily: 'We have nothing that can kill a tiger, nothing. Nothing at all.'

'There is a way.' Navarr's eyes were hard. 'A way I read about once. The way the *tigeros* hunt killer jaguars in the Brazilian forests.'

'How's that?' Rex looked dubious.

'It's simply done. They hunt with a long spear, deliberately going into country where they know the brute lies up, and using themselves as bait. When the big cats attack they simply jam the blunt end of the spear into the ground and let the cat land on the point. Its own weight drives the spear home. Then you hang on until the cat dies, keeping the length of the spear between you so the brute can't touch you with its claws. It's a dangerous technique, but it works.'

'No!' Lorretta spoke sharply. 'It's too dangerous. I've heard of the *tigeros*, but they are all native hunters, Indians who know exactly what they're doing. No amateur could do it.'

Navarr met her eyes. He said simply: 'If it isn't killed it will pick us off one by one. And I'd rather go down fighting.'

'Steve you can't — '

Navarr pulled his gaze away from the appeal in her blue eyes. He said grimly: 'I'm going to need a long stout pole.

Something about ten foot long, and two or three inches thick. Give me a hand to find one, Rex. Schelde can watch the women.'

★ ★ ★

From a vantage point high up on a rocky hillside the waiting shape of the crippled cat watched the small party of humans moving along the bottom of a ravine. The sun was high above and he had waited a long time for them to come this way. He had trailed them throughout the previous night and had then circled the hated fire to lie in wait ahead of them. Now his white jaws slavered in anticipation. There were four of them close together in the lead, but the fifth, a man, hung back alone, almost a hundred yards behind, carrying a long pointed pole. The burning eyes picked on the straggler. Blazing with hate the great cat recognised the man who had thrust fire into his face. The great tawny shape bounded swiftly and suddenly down the hillside, circling round to approach the far end of the ravine.

There was a dense thicket of fern and jasmine there, choking the boles of a group of palms. The cat reached it well ahead of his quarry and flattened in the dense shadows. The palm fronds sheltered him from the heat of the sun, and the heady scent of jasmine filled the air. The old cat waited, his sleek body merging with the colours around him.

He watched the first four move past him, moving doggedly through the heat haze that filled the ravine. A long way behind the straggler followed. The cat watched the tall, lean-faced man come nearer, saw the sweat glistening on his bare chest where his jacket hung open, saw his face, black and shiny beneath his hat, more sweat running into the stubble that clothed the hard jaw. He saw too the long pointed spear, the sharpened end black where it had been hardened in the dying fire.

That pole puzzled the cat. He eyed it warily, his instinct giving him faint warning of the danger in that simple pole. But he was too hungry to let vague caution turn him aside. It was three days since his last kill. He watched and waited. The man drew ever nearer, and the sleek muscles tensed for the charge. The gleaming eyes blazed and the tail swished gently. Bunching back on three legs the crippled feline uttered a fearsome roar, and sprang straight at the hated man before him.

13

Another Death

The spear that Navarr carried was nearly eleven feet long and some three inches thick, and already the weight of it was proving a burden. It dragged behind him and pulled at his arms, causing him to lag even farther behind the others than he intended. Several times he saw Lorretta turn and look at him, but she never spoke. She had argued and pleaded all the while he was fashioning his spear, but to no avail. Rex had remained sceptical, and Schelde nervous. Ruth Ballard had shown no interest.

Now Navarr was alone, waiting for the cat to attack while the others remained in a protective bunch up ahead. He had no fear that the animal would attack the others rather than himself, for the brute's hereditary sense of caution would lead it to pick upon the only straggler, Navarr was sure of that. If the cat was still stalking them, and he was certain that it was, then he would be the selected victim. He only hoped that the cat would appear soon. For an hour or two he would be alert and ready, but if the tiger held off until later in the day he would be weary, and easily taken by surprise. Besides, he wanted to get it over.

He was sweating freely as he walked, and he knew that it was not all due to the sun. Deep inside he was afraid. But not only afraid for himself — there was so much more at stake than his own life. The rest of the party would soon break up without someone to hold them together, and although Rex might carry on and make an attempt to lead, Navarr had his doubts. Rex was just as liable to break first. Navarr knew exactly what the odds were. If he died, then the others would be lost, and the last hope for the thousands of Nakai would be gone. Navarr had translated Larrieux's dying phrase into new words now. 'One must survive' had become '*I* must survive,' for without him the others would be lost anyway. He kept thinking of those words as he walked. He had to survive, had to get out of this jungle waste alive. But first he had to kill the stalking tiger.

The sun was hot on his back as they neared the far end of the ravine. The jungle clung thickly to the rock and earth of the high walls, but in the centre it was fairly easy travelling. The wild splendour of a burning carpet of red and orange orchids caught his eye where they spilled across the ravine floor. They scintillated in a blaze of glory in the sunlight, but he forced his attention away. He had to keep his whole mind on the crippled tiger. It could be lurking anywhere, and to relax even for a moment might prove fatal.

He kept his eyes away from the beauty of the orchids and moved on. His hands were slippery on the shaft of his spear, the hard black point jerked as he walked. He saw the clump of fern and jasmine that clustered beneath the palm grove. The jasmine smelt sweet in the morning air, and he wished that he had the time to enjoy it. He grew level with the clump and then, like a snarling tornado, the crippled cat charged.

The roar brought Navarr swinging round to face it. He saw the bared jaws and blazing eyes hurtling down on him. The great cat's claws were unsheathed and stretched towards him as it leapt. He saw the white belly as it arched upwards and then the snarling terror was looming above him and crashing down. He swung the spear round and leaned back on it, gritting his teeth as he held the fire-hardened point directly beneath the descending brute. The spear-point crashed through the great chest and brought a shrieking scream of rage from the agonised cripple. The great weight hurled the spear to one side and dragged Navarr over with it. One razor-edged paw flailed past within inches of his face. Desperately Navarr clung on to his spear. The point had penetrated almost a foot into the cat's chest just below the throat but still the brute fought as it died. It writhed and clawed like an exploding coil of snarling, spitting steel. Its screaming snarls of pain echoed in blood-curdling shrieks through the ravine. Navarr was whipped and flung from side to side like a leaf in a storm. Still he hung on, bruised and bleeding, but still keeping the length of the spear between himself and the taloned paws of the dying cat. Then, as was inevitable, the unbarbed spear jerked free.

The cat flung itself away, blood drenching the white stomach from the great hole in its chest. Screaming, it flung itself forward in one last savage charge. Navarr swung his spear like a long club, smashing the bloodied point against the leaping cat's jaws and at the same time throwing himself aside. The cripple landed just beyond him and he squirmed around in the dirt to face it. His whole frame was tensed to roll again but the cat had made its last great effort. It had collapsed on one side as it landed and lay writhing in the grip of approaching death.

Navarr got to his feet and ran frantically out of range of the dying claws. His foot caught in a root and he crashed over and lay still. He almost screamed at the horrifying thought that the tiger might land on his back. But the old cripple was dead.

Navarr lay there trembling in a sweat of fear, the after effects sapping his will to move now that it was over. He felt one mass of grazed and aching bruises from the battering he had received, his head was ringing and he could taste blood in his mouth where his lip had split. His ribs had taken a terrible hammering as he hung on to the flailing shaft of the spear and felt as tender as raw meat. Half of his jacket had been torn away and he had lost his hat. He felt as dead as the great cat behind him and Rex and Lorretta had to lift him up bodily when they came running back to the scene. Both their faces were white, and Lorretta's eyes were terrified.

'Steve! Steve!' She was shouting the words hysterically. 'Steve, are you all right?'

He forced a grin, a ghastly, bloody-lipped, mask of a grin.

'Hell no!' he croaked. 'I think I've bust my braces.'

She stared at him. Then the words sank

265

in and she realised that not even a death duel with a tiger could change him. She began to cry.

Navarr rallied his strength then. He shrugged Rex away and laid one arm across her shoulders. For a moment he fumbled for something to say.

'How do you fancy tiger steaks?' he asked at last.

She looked up and blinked the last tears out of her eyes.

'Tiger steaks?' She looked amazed. And then she laughed, just a trifle hysterical still.

Schelde reached them with Ruth Ballard and stared at the bloodied arena with the dead cat sprawling in the centre. The animal's twisted forepaw lay outstretched, almost touching the great spear. The eyes were still open but the green fire was dulled.

'Miraculous! Impossible!' Schelde said. He entered the trampled clearing tentatively to retrieve Navarr's hat. He came back with it in his hand and held it out. 'Miraculous,' he said again. 'I admit, Mr. Navarr, that I did not think you could do it. It is most remarkable.'

Rex eyed the dead cat. 'Me too, Navarr, I thought you were crazy. I guess I was wrong.'

Navarr sat down weakly on the ground, his stomach was still whirling and the reaction of the battle was sweeping over him in a rising flood. He fumbled in his pocket and pulled out the knife. He flicked it open and handed it to Rex.

'Cut as much meat as we can carry from the haunches,' he said grimly. 'But be careful, the nerves might make it kick.'

Lorretta looked startled. 'You're really serious. I thought you were kidding.'

Navarr forced another grin. 'It's the law of the jungle, our crippled friend wouldn't have had any hesitation about what to do if I'd lost. Besides, with our resources we can't afford to pick and choose. We'll eat any meat that comes up.'

They watched as Rex cautiously approached the dead tiger, keeping well clear of the limp paws. He jabbed it with the knife and then cut half a dozen heavy portions of meat from the haunch and shoulder. The body was still warm and the job of butchering made his face go pale beneath his thick blond beard.

They left the carcass to the vultures, gleaming-eyed, hook-beaked scavengers that moved in before they had travelled fifty yards. Once clear of the ravine and its death-tainted air, they stopped to roast the meat before it rotted. Here they ate their heartiest meal since leaving Nakai, and then divided what was left into six large portions that the men could carry easily in their jacket pockets. The portions were well wrapped up in large leaves, and they were now well supplied with food for several days. Their major problem was water, there being little more than three inches left in the bottom of their bag.

The terrain of Burma remained always the same as they trekked on, obstacle following obstacle. Navarr was nearly always in the lead now, forging determinedly ahead, pushing himself to the limit. Once Lorretta had to stop him, gasping urgently: 'Ease up, Steve, the others can't keep the pace.'

He stopped to look back, the other three had dropped well behind.

'Sorry,' he said lamely. 'I didn't realise I was pulling ahead.'

She smiled wearily. 'Pulling ahead? you were practically racing.' She hesitated. 'You shouldn't drive yourself so hard. We'll make it.'

Something of the trust in her tone brought a new confidence to his heart. He found the energy to grin. 'Sure we'll make it. And when we do I'm going to take you out to dinner. I'm going to take you to the smartest night club in town, and we're going to drink champagne until we've worn out the glasses. Then we'll take a drive by moonlight, and after that I'm going to make love to you.' He made it a statement, calm and a matter of fact.

She smiled again. 'Please, Steve. I'd like that.' She meant every word.

A few seconds later Schelde, Rex, and Ruth Ballard, caught them up and they moved on. While they walked they had no energy for talking.

The sun was dropping behind them

now, throwing their shadows forward to lead the way. They walked like drunks, with their heads down to watch their path, and none of them noticed the sudden clouds that appeared in the north. Black and menacing they rolled up from the horizon, like the incoming tide of an angry sea, rushing over the white glaring shore of the sky. Within a matter of minutes the whole of the northern skyline was blotted out by the black masses of cloud. Dark and sullen, touched with edgings of purple, they moved in over the jungle hills.

The sudden dullness as the clouds moved overhead shocked the five survivors to a standstill. Navarr stared up as the sun vanished from view and the whole earth was thrown into shadow.

'Storm!' he exclaimed bitterly. 'I might have guessed it. It's about the only bloody thing we haven't had so far.'

Rex watched the clouds swallow up more of the gradually diminishing patches of clear sky. 'It's going to be one helluva storm too. We'd best find shelter.'

Navarr glanced round grimly. They

were surrounded by low jungle and vegetation but over to their left was a green-flanked hillside. Through the green of the foliage he could see the grey granite of rocks. He turned towards it. 'Let's get over there. We might be able to find an overhang or something on that hillside, it looks rocky enough.'

There was nothing else around that might possibly offer them a better choice, and they struggled through the barrier of jungle towards the hillside that Navarr had indicated. They hurried as best they could as the clouds completely filled the sky, casting a gloomy dusk over the earth. Quite abruptly a single lance of rain splashed down on the leaves near Lorretta's face, another lance, and then another, spearing down in vicious slender streaks. The foliage quailled and then the whole world blackened and was cut from view by the driving curtain of solid rain. The downpour soaked them through within seconds and beat like giant hailstones on their backs.

They crashed through the wet, splashing undergrowth and started up the slope of the hill, peering through the fury of the storm with half-closed eyes. Navarr found Lorretta and clamped one arm about her shoulders, dragging her stumbling and slipping by his side. Rex cursed and swore as he followed them up the slope, while Schelde gritted his teeth and blindly hustled Ruth Ballard along. The roar and hiss of the descending rain was like the growl of a mighty waterfall in their ears. The ground became mud beneath their feet and the force of the cloudburst stung like countless swarms of diving hornets on their shoulders. It was like forcing their way through a vertical curtain of thin, downward concentrated jets. The tree tops flailed in the wind and the whipping branches lashed their faces and bodies as they fought their way on.

Desperately Navarr kept going until Rex suddenly yelled from somewhere to their left. He still had his arm around Lorretta and he realised with a sudden surge of alarm that he had become separated from the other three in the storm. He turned on a new track across the flank of the hillside and followed the distorted sound of the American's voice. He slipped into the mud and the rain almost nailed him to the ground before he staggered up. He dragged Lorretta on and then suddenly there was a wall of rock before him. There was a high horizontal crack at the base and Rex was sitting inside, he had both hands to his mouth and was shouting loudly.

Navarr half turned to look for Schelde and in the same moment the little Belgian blundered into him in the near-darkness, he was still hanging on to Ruth Ballard. Together they thrust the two women into the low shelter and then moved in behind them. The rain closed like a veil behind them and they sat weekly on the bare rock, water streaming down their faces and bodies. The crack in the rock was about five feet high and three times as long. It only penetrated for four or five feet, the roof sloping down all the time, but as the rain outside was practically vertical they were still sheltered in the shallow cave mouth.

Lorretta leaned back weakly, fighting to regain her breath. Her ragged skirt had been ripped to the hip during their frantic flight through the storm and now the whole length of her left leg was bared to the thigh. Her wet blouse was plastered close to the skin, close and revealing enough to leave her as good as naked above the waist in the dull grey light. Her hair was soaked and stuck limply to her face. She began to shiver and pulled her open costume jacket closer about her.

Navarr glanced around and saw that Ruth Ballard was in pretty much the same state. Rex and Schelde, too, were shaking a little as the cooling rainwater ran down their bare chests. Navarr realised grimly that unless they built a fire and dried out it was quite likely that they would all finish up with a serious attack of fever before the next morning. Another thought struck him in the same moment and the new realisation was by far the most important. They needed water; and here were hundreds of tons of it shooting away to waste.

He shrugged out of his jacket quickly and unzipped the water bag to remove the empty flask casing. With a brief explanation to answer Lorretta's sudden query he moved out again into the sheeting storm.

The flailing rain hit like a thousand lashes on his naked back as he staggered out to the nearest bushes. He almost yelped with the stinging pain, and his fingers were hurried and clumsy as he tied his jacket by the sleeves and two corners to some of the stouter branches. The jacket ballooned downwards as the driving water began to fill up in the centre and he dropped on his knees to position the tin beneath it. He gritted his teeth as the rain struck out with renewed fury at his bare flesh and steadied the tin in the earth where it could catch the thin trickle of water that was already running through the cloth of his coat. Leaving it he ran back to the shelter of the cave.

He gave it several minutes and then ran back to find the tin full and brimming over. He emptied it into their water bag and replaced it beneath his jacket. Schelde applauded with brief nods, while Rex sprawled back exhausted. Lorretta was still shivering, for the sudden change of temperature was unnaturally cold. Water was dripping all around their rocky shelter.

Navarr kept on filling his tin until he had refilled the water bag completely. By then almost an hour had passed and still the solid curtain of rain lashed down. A shrieking wind was flailing the palms and tree tops and the sound of the storm was a continuous roar of sound. Navarr retrieved his sodden jacket and crawled back into the cave mouth.

Schelde was watching the rain curtain the entrance and said sadly: 'This is bad, very bad.'

Navarr grinned. 'It's not so bad. We're okay for water again, and tomorrow it will be just as hot.'

'You do not understand.' Schelde sounded worried. 'This is Burma. Here, when the rainy season starts, it continues in deluge after deluge for several months. Once it starts the mosquitoes become thick as the leaves. Malaria and other diseases are always here. This jungle will become a sodden hell. We shall never get out.'

Navarr slapped him on the shoulder. 'The monsoon doesn't set in properly until June, now it's only mid-May. This is only a freak storm.'

'I think not. I think the rainy season has set in early. Our chances now are slim, very slim. No chance at all.'

Navarr grinned. Despite the cold he was feeling more cheerful now that their water bag was again full. 'We'll make it,' he said confidently. 'But right now we'd better get out there while we can still see and get in some firewood. We need a fire to dry out, and it'll soon be night, anyway.'

Schelde looked out into the rain reluctantly. 'I suppose you are right.' He began to get up.

Navarr pulled on his soaking jacket to protect his skin from the full force of the storm as he stepped outside. He glanced back to where Rex still lay weakly in the cave. 'Come on, Rex, you too.'

The American looked up. 'Like hell!' he said sullenly. 'I'll go out when the rain stops, but not before.'

'The rain might last all night and we need a fire.'

'Then make one, Buddy, but count me out. I'm damned if I'm going out in that. I'd rather stay wet.' There was an arrogant twist to his mouth again, and he moved farther back into the cave.

Navarr said flatly: 'You're getting out. Move!' His black, streaming face was hard and angry.

'Look, Mister, for once I've had enough of being ordered about. All right, so you're a good guy. You kill tigers every day. You're a real hardcase. But that still don't make you lord-God-Almighty.' Rex's anger stemmed from weariness and at the moment he was just past caring. He went on: 'If I figured I needed a fire I'd make one. But I don't. I'm okay just sitting in the dry, that's good enough for me. And you can go to hell.'

Navarr glanced at Lorretta who was still shivering slightly. 'She needs a fire, she's going to get feverish without one.'

'Well, she's your woman. You build her one.'

'What the hell does that mean?' Navarr

sounded dangerous.

'What it says, you were playing lover boy last night. You take care of her.'

Navarr stiffened, one hand closed in a fist and his eyes were steel-hard. He looked black and ugly against a background of sheeting rain and the roar of the storm. Schelde touched his arm nervously.

'Please, please, it is no use to argue.'

Navarr glared at Rex. 'Are you getting out to help us, or do I have to throw you out?'

Rex half sat up. 'Still the hardcase? Well listen, Buddy, if I don't wanta go out in that rain then nobody's gonna make me.'

Navarr lunged into the cave but Lorretta caught his arm before his fingers could close over the American's jacket.

'No, Steve, no! Fighting isn't going to help. I'll give you a hand to gather wood.'

Navarr stopped, his outstretched hand still reaching towards Rex. 'Why should you, when there's another man here to do it? Why should he skulk and take it easy?'

'Come on, Steve, come on!' She tugged desperately and pulled him upright in the cave mouth. 'Come on, the three of us can manage.'

Navarr hesitated. If Schelde had tried to pull him back he would have thrown the little man aside and then hurled Rex out after him. But Lorretta was different. She was clinging on to him like a limpet, and while he hesitated some of his black rage died.

He turned sourly and she led him away into the storm-threshed jungle. Schelde moved off in a parallel line, while Rex watched them go with sullen eyes.

Sticking together with the rain beating around them Lorretta and Navarr gathered armfuls of branches and dried bamboo husks for a fire. They fought their way back to the cave and dumped them just inside. Rex watched without moving and again Lorretta had practically to drag the lean-faced newspaper-man away from the cave. They passed Schelde, who had an armful of wood, but the shrieks of the storm made it impossible to speak. The density of the rain was making it almost as black as night. The jungle was writhing and flapping beneath the impact of wind and rain.

They slipped and stumbled through the muddy slope of the hillside as they gathered a second arm load of wood. Then as they turned to move back to the cave Lorretta slipped on to her knees. Navarr dropped his load and used both hands to help her up. Her clothes were plastered about her and her hair was a be-draggled mess. Her full breasts were almost bared where her blouse had broken open and her eyes were suddenly wild as she stared up at him. She clung to him suddenly and their wet bodies seemed to adhere together as she crushed herself against him.

'Kiss me, Steve! I've never been kissed in the rain.'

He kissed her, hungrily, violently. The rain streamed down their faces and parted around their locked mouths, beating on them in a frenzy of frustrated rage as they clung together. Navarr felt her breasts, cold and wet on his chest. He crushed her slim body in his great arms, and felt her wet lips quiver with desire against his mouth.

Then from out of the storm they heard a rumbling crash and above it a shrieking scream from Ruth Ballard.

They stopped, mouths parted but their bodies still merged together. Then in the same moment they started back at a blind staggering run through the rain to their cave, their heaps of firewood forgotten in the mud.

They found the cave blocked by a landslide of earth and boulders that the storm had loosened and sent crashing down the hillside. It had hit and half buried the two members of their party who had stayed inside.

Ruth Ballard was alive, but moaning in pain.

Leo Rex was dead.

14

Three Alone

Schelde rejoined them seconds later, his dumpy body moving jerkily as he blundered through the rain-beaten undergrowth, in his arms he carried a mound of firewood. His feet slithered in the mud and he only just regained his balance as he brought himself to a halt beside them.

A sizeable portion of the hillside had tumbled down to almost obliterate the cave mouth that was their only shelter. Rex had apparently tried to spring clear and had caught the full weight of the slide as he ran out; his big body was half-buried, the legs and waist invisible in the fallen avalanche of rubble; there was blood on the side of his unshaven face and his hat had fallen clear of the debris; the back of his jacket was torn and a great, bleeding bruise showed where a falling boulder had broken his back before rolling away.

From the other side of the fall, inside the cave, they could still hear Ruth Ballard moaning. They could see no sign of her but the moans told them that she was alive.

Without hesitation Navarr plunged straight into the task of clearing the fall. He clawed desperately at the rock and rubble, hurling the larger lumps aside. Schelde and Lorretta needed no urging and within seconds all three were working like Trojans in the streaming rain. They had no energy to waste on speech, and as they worked, the only sounds were the harsh gasping of their breathing and the snarling fury of the storm, punctuated by moans from the injured woman in the cave. Within minutes their hands were bleeding and their nails broken. Lorretta swore every time she snagged her fingers and Schelde uttered little yelps of pain. Navarr worked in savage, unrelenting silence. None of them paused to rest.

It took them an hour of back-breaking work to clear the great mound of earth and rock and reach the still figure of Ruth Ballard, an hour of strength-sapping labour, during which the torrential rain never once eased up; an hour of scrambling blindly like rats at a mud heap. And when they did finally uncover her the moans had stopped, and she lay as silent as the grave.

She lay on her face and once they had cleared the debris that buried the lower half of her body they turned her over gently. Lorretta examined her slowly, running her hands cautiously over the still and muddied form. They had worked their way into the cave and outside the rain still fell in a solid curtain.

Lorretta looked up at last. Her wet face was streaked with plastered hair and her eyes were dull and uncertain. 'There are no bones broken,' she said. 'But from the way she was moaning she must have been in pain before she passed out. I think she must have internal injuries. There was a lot of weight on her stomach.'

Navarr said nothing. The beating rain and the tiring work of clearing the avalanche had left him too exhausted to voice the bitter thoughts that filled his mind.

Schelde said anxiously: 'Is there nothing we can do?'

Lorretta looked at him and shook her head.

'What could we do? We don't even know where she's hurt.' Her voice was weary.

Navarr pushed himself to his feet, out of the cave.

'We'll get the fire going,' he said. 'Then we'll bury Rex.' He could feel the savage force of the rain flaying his back, and finished: 'We shall have to stay in the cave, if there was anything else loose up there the first fall would have brought it down. And anyway, until we know how badly she's hurt we daren't move her. It might kill her.' He glanced at Schelde. 'Get on with the fire will you? I'll see if I can find the wood we dropped.'

Without waiting for an answer he turned and squelched across the muddy hillside, and in an instant he was swallowed up by the storm. It took him ten minutes to find the twin bundles of wood that he and Lorretta had gathered; ten minutes of slithering through the mud and avoiding wind-whipped branches and wet tangles of vegetation. He found them, and carried them back to the half-cleared cave one at a time. He hardly noticed the downpour now, for although the storm was still at its height it had become like the jungle, a constant and demanding enemy, which had to be ignored to be defeated.

That night was the worst they had yet spent. First they had to bury Rex, for by morning the jackals might have discovered his corpse. It was grim work, carried out while the storm raged about them. The few words that Navarr spoke over the grave were torn away by the wind and lost in the roaring black void of falling water. For the rest of the night they listened to Ruth Ballard's delirious moaning. The injured woman's face was white and bloodless, and it soon became clear that she suffered from some kind of internal injuries. Pain twisted her features, and many times she called out the name of her dead husband.

Lorretta sat and smoothed the sweat from the shining face. Schelde watched her helplessly. Navarr stared into the black, storming night, facing up to the hardest decision he had ever been forced to make. It was clear that Ruth Ballard was in no condition to be moved, yet every day he delayed for her was another day in which Voron could enact his grim plot to destroy the mighty U.S. air base at Nakai. On the face of it, the choice should have been simple enough. But it wasn't. The inhabitants of Nakai were just statistics in his mind, theoretical numbers too distant to be appreciated as flesh and blood; whereas the injured woman lying not two yards away was fierce reality, a member of his own party, a woman who had shared the same dangers as himself. Her life was one he had fought to save when he faced the crippled cat along the bloodied length of his spear, and it was not a life he could relinquish easily. For a moment he thought of going on alone, leaving Lorretta and Schelde to tend her until he could send help. But they had only one water bag, one knife, one bow. Because of that he couldn't split them up.

All night he struggled with his decision, facing it alone, for that had always been his nature. And through it all he could see no answer. They had to move on, but they couldn't leave Ruth Ballard. Yet to try and move her would probably kill her.

Dawn came as a cold grey light that gleamed wetly on the dripping trees. The storm had finally passed, but its path was well marked by broken branches and palm fronds, torn down by the fury of the wind. The sun climbed slowly, and soon the wet foliage began to sparkle with little twinkles of silver-green. The jungle began to steam in the heat. Ruth Ballard still lay close to death, her face beneath the tangled white hair was pale and bloodless. None of the other three had slept.

The morning passed, with Lorretta continually nursing the injured woman. Schelde watched her miserably. Navarr sat in the cave mentally exhausted. He had finally capitulated to his problem and decided to wait another day. Perhaps by tomorrow she would be well enough to talk, and once he knew how badly she was hurt he could decide whether or not to risk making some kind of stretcher with which to carry her. He justified his decision with the fact that all three of them needed a rest, anyway. This was their ninth day in the jungle, and he could only hope that Voron too was meeting with difficulties and delays.

Towards mid-day Schelde relieved Lorretta of the job of watching the unconscious woman, and she moved wearily out of the cave into the sunlight. Her whole body ached from sitting, and it was a painful luxury just to straighten her bowed shoulders. After a while Navarr joined her. Her eyes were heavy, and her blonde hair showed auburn streaks where the rain had washed the dye away. She pushed her hair back self-consciously.

'I look a sight, don't I?'

'Yes,' Navarr agreed. 'You look a hell of a sight. But in the circumstances I guess most women would look worse.'

'Even with the dye running?' Her hand strayed to her hair again.

'Sure! Those merging colours look cute. You ought to leave it permanent.'

She smiled. 'Thanks, Steve! You couldn't know how much that means.' The smile broadened. 'You look pretty good too, kind of attractively fearsome.'

He grinned. 'That's the first time I've been called that — attractive, I mean.' He glanced at the cave and his mood changed suddenly. 'What do you think? Will she live?'

'I don't know, Steve.' Her voice was hesitant. 'She's hurt inside. Out here there's just nothing we can do.'

Navarr's lean face became black and ugly again. 'So she'll die too — all of them, one by one, they just keep falling away — we've left nothing but a trail of graves half way across bloody Burma. What with rivers, man-eaters, and a blasted murderer among — ' He stopped there suddenly. There were so many other, more pressing dangers that he had almost forgotten that there had been a murderer among them.

Lorretta stared horrified into his eyes, the same thought having stirred in her mind the moment he so abruptly stopped speaking. She said slowly: 'Steve, you don't think — '

'Damn it! I don't know what to think.' He shot a sharp glance into the cave where Schelde still knelt over Ruth Ballard, then grabbed hold of Lorretta and hustled her out of the little man's hearing. He said grimly: 'It's possible. He could have started that landslide, and he could be the one who killed the two airmen and Asaka.' Navarr's face was haggard. 'Hell! This is a bloody nightmare. The killer might have been any of those three men who died by accident, Dorapho, Rex, or Chang Lee. Or that fall might not have been an accident. The killer could be Schelde.'

Lorretta looked doubtful. 'But he was in love with Ruth, I'm sure of that. Look at the way he's cared for her, he's never left her. I don't think he could kill her.'

Navarr almost groaned. It was hard to imagine anyone like Schelde being in love, but love was an emotion that knew no levels. And Lorretta was right; Schelde had helped the ailing Englishwoman every foot of the way. At last he said weakly:

'It could be an act. She's too weak and helpless to be any danger to Voron's schemes. He just might be using her to fool us.'

'No,' she said stubbornly. 'He pulled her out of the plane — remember? And now he's in love with her. I know he is.'

Navarr said quietly: 'I'm going to check. If he did climb up the hill and start that landslide then there may be footprints. I'm going to take a look.'

'All right then, I'll come with you.'

Together they circled round to the back of the cave, pushing a path through the jungle and up the rocky hillside. They found the point where the slide had started and searched around for several minutes but they could find nothing to indicate that Schelde might have climbed up there the night before. There was plenty of loose rock lying about, and it was clear that a good push could easily have been the cause of the landslide. However, the rain could have loosened the earth to start one just as easily, and any sign that there might have been foul play was washed away by the downpour which had turned parts of the ground into a muddy swamp. There was no way of knowing what had really happened.

They returned to the cave and said nothing. Schelde looked up sadly as they came in. 'She still moans,' he said miserably. 'She cries for Howard, always for Howard.'

Navarr was baffled, and didn't know how to answer.

The day dragged on as the sun continued its scorching journey across the sky, the shadows moved round slowly. The jungle had long since stopped steaming, but it still had the fresh quality of greenness. The distant mountains to the west had clarified into a dull purple barrier against the skyline. The white clouds of morning had gone, and the sky was a glaring blue dome of reflected heat.

Finally, late in the afternoon, Ruth Ballard came out of her coma. Her moans became more constant and at last she opened her eyes. 'Howard,' she said weakly. 'Howard!'

They could get nothing else out of her until suddenly she croaked: 'I'm cold. Cold.'

Carefully Navarr and Schelde covered her with their jackets, and she became silent again. Navarr rebuilt the fire near her, wondering how long she would last. He heard her moan as he worked, and suddenly every shred of reason vanished as he made his decision. Nakai or no Nakai he just couldn't leave her. He would make a stretcher that he and Schelde could carry, and take her with them. It was the only way.

Navarr told Lorretta and Schelde what he intended, and they both nodded in assent. He took his knife and left the cave again to cut poles for a stretcher. He had a vague idea of stringing vines between them to make a sort of rope ladder affair that could be covered with palm fronds. He wasn't at all sure how he meant to accomplish this, but he worked on the assumption that he could figure something out once he had the materials in his hands.

Back in the cave Ruth had recovered a little, but she was still in pain. She was shivering with fever despite a blazing fire, and Lorretta and Schelde were taking it in turns to sit with her. Lorretta was nursing her head and trying to get her to talk in order to revive her spirits, but when she finally succeeded the conversation turned the wrong way.

Ruth said weakly: 'I've been a burden to you, haven't I? All the way I've been slowing you up.'

'Of course not! We don't mind waiting for you.'

'You do. You're trying to be kind, but you do.' Her lips moved very slowly. 'You see, I heard what that Frenchman said when he died. I know why you have to get — ' She choked hoarsely.

Lorretta smoothed the sweat from her temples. 'All right now, don't talk if you don't want to.'

'But I do want to . . . now. I — I suppose I'm selfish really. All I've ever thought of since he — since he died, was Howard. I never thought about any of you, just poor Howard.'

'We understand. Don't try to talk.'

'Got to — got to talk now. You see, I know — I know what you're thinking. I can't walk any more. I'm dying. But you have to go on . . . you have to go on because of all those people on that island.' Her limbs stiffened in pain and her hands moved jerkily beneath Navarr's coat. Sweat broke out again on her forehead as she went on: 'You can't take me with you, can you? You've got to leave me.'

'We won't leave you. Steve is making a stretcher now. We're going to carry you.' Lorretta spoke the words reassuringly.

'No,' a ghost of a smile twisted the weak lips. 'No, they need their strength — to get out, not to carry a . . . dead woman. I've been selfish too long. I suppose really — in one way — I'm still being selfish now.' The elderly face smiled. 'You see . . . I'm going to join Howard. Good-bye, my dear. And thank you.'

The roar of a gun sounded sharp and clear through the cave and Ruth Ballard's body jerked violently. Her head rolled from Lorretta's lap with the eyes closed as the echoes rang through the rocks.

Lorretta stared down dumbly, hearing Navarr yell aloud as he crashed back towards the cave. He reached it just as Schelde found the will to move and tore the coat away from the upper part of Ruth's body. Ruth held Larrieux's tiny automatic in her right hand. She'd thrust the snub nose beneath her left breast before she fired, her blouse was red with blood and blackened by the powder burn. The bullet had penetrated her heart after a journey of some three inches.

Schelde took the gun from her nerveless fingers and looked up at Navarr.

'Your gun!' His voice rang with an almost savage hysteria. 'She took your gun from the pocket of your jacket.'

Slowly, dazedly, Navarr turned away. He stared down the hillside into the green barrier of the jungle where the half-finished stretcher lay on the ground. For long moments he stood there, teeth and fists clenched tight. Then, bitterly, he went to retrieve his knife.

15

A Close Call

They buried Ruth Ballard before the sun had set, laying her beside Rex, and covering her face with the old black hat she had worn before they packed rocks and soil around her. The sun threw long, grim shadows from the heaped-up graves as Navarr again spoke the few words of the burial service that now came so effortlessly to his tongue. They were all sweating still in the heat. Lorretta looked haggard, as though she would cry if only the sun had not sucked the moisture she might have used for tears through the pores of her skin. Schelde looked strangely lost and alone, his pork-pie hat held to his bare, dirt-streaked chest.

When it was finished, they returned to the shade of their hole in the rocks. The setting sun was a glorious parade of flashing colours as it sank behind the red-purple haze of the western mountains, but none of them watched it go down. There were just the three of them now — three out of eleven.

They ate another tasteless supper, washed down with a mouthful of the tepid water from their bag. Then, as night closed in and spared them the discouraging prospect of having to sit and stare dumbly at the graves of their friends, they slept. This time Navarr set no watches. They needed their sleep and he doubted the possibility of anything disturbing them while the fire was going, and since Kay Leonard had died he found that he now woke automatically once the fire began to fade. Even when there was someone on watch he would wake, the instinct to survive over-ruling all others now that the danger had been brought home. He knew that he would not sleep when the fire went out.

Several times he awoke when the fire began to cool and heaped more wood on the embers. Once his eyes rested for a long time on Schelde and he wondered how big a chance he was taking by sleeping when there was just a possibility that the little man was a killer. Despite Lorretta's certainty, he still wasn't sure. Schelde's sorrow seemed sincere enough over Ruth's death, but he might still be playing a part. He finally shrugged his thoughts aside and lay down to sleep, certain in his own mind that he would awaken if Schelde were to move, for the truth was that he was subconsciously listening all the while. Even when he slept, his senses were alert for any hint of treachery.

The following morning they moved off again. Navarr leading the way with the bow over his shoulder and the arrows stuck in his belt. Lorretta carried a bird he had shot the day before, while Schelde carried the water bag. Navarr was still worried about Schelde, he only had to up-end that water bag and they were finished. But it would also finish him, so the fact that he tried nothing of the kind failed to prove his innocence. It might only mean that he was waiting for some other way which would leave him a hope of survival. That was, if he *was* the killer; they still had no way of knowing.

They were travelling a little faster now, but not much, for both their spirits and their energy were badly sapped. Navarr still had his watch, and they moved by walking for an hour and then resting for ten minutes. Mid-day found them crossing fairly level ground beneath high trees which closed out the sunlight fifty feet above them. The undergrowth was dense, and the heat humid. Everything smelt dank, and breathing was like drawing warm steam into their lungs. They rested and swallowed a mouthful of water each, a tiny drop that just moistened their leathery throats and was gone.

Lorretta said wearily: 'I don't think we're ever going to get out of this. The jungle keeps on and on for ever, and our numbers keep getting cut down. And the fewer of us there are, the higher the odds against survival.'

Schelde said moodily: 'We have been unlucky, very unlucky! Perhaps it will change.'

Lorretta lay back in the wet under-growth, revelling momentarily in the coolness as the dampness touched her skin through her clothes.

'Luck!' she said bitterly. 'Yes, I guess you could say we are unlucky. Too unlucky. We've just about had it.'

Navarr gave her a black grin. 'We'll make it! We must have covered well over sixty miles by now. Just stick it another two or three days. We must stumble into a native village soon, or else reach the Irrawaddy.'

Their eyes met as they lay side by side. 'I'll stick it,' she said softly. 'As long as you're with me, I'll stick it.'

Her eyes offered all the invitation he needed and he pulled himself towards her. Gently he kissed her on the mouth.

'Good girl!' he said. 'We'll paint the town red yet.'

Her hand came up tentatively to caress his bearded cheeks, and she felt the bristles rasp against her fingers. 'Kiss me again, Steve,' she pleaded. 'But do it softly, these aren't exactly smooth and fluffy.'

He kissed her again, tenderly, and then lay beside her beneath the high awning of tree-tops. Behind them Schelde lay silent, as if half asleep, and they rested for a long time before moving.

At last they got up to file on through the nightmare world of heat and close-tangled jungle, sweating and staggering in a half-numbed state where the mind was a vacuum and their bodies only moved because that was the accepted routine. The mosquitoes seemed thicker than ever before, and Navarr wondered how long it would be before one or all of them went down with malaria. Both Schelde and Lorretta were looking feverish after the soaking they had endured two nights before.

He kept his thoughts to himself, however, stumbling blindly on, moving one foot slowly in front of the other . . . then the next . . . then the first foot again . . . wiping away the sweat . . . pushing aside vegetation . . . ducking beneath branches . . . one foot in front of the other . . . sweating . . . on and on . . . on and on . . . bring up the next foot . . . wipe away the sweat. On and on and on.

After another two to three hours of marching, they stumbled into a small grass-carpeted clearing which made an ideal camp-site.

There was still an hour or so of daylight left, but the state of his companions caused Navarr to call a halt. Both were showing feverish signs, and Schelde in particular looked bad. Several times during the day Navarr had seen him seized with a bout of shivering, and it was clear that the little man was ill. It was something he should have expected really, the effect of malnutrition, jungle, and storm, had to show sooner or later. Navarr was only surprised that Lorretta was not seriously ill as well.

Hurriedly Navarr got the fire going, refusing the little Belgian's game offer to help him gather wood. He knew that Schelde was going to be a lot sicker before morning, and he didn't want to sap the little man's strength.

He was right. He roasted the plover he had shot the day before and had practically to force Schelde to swallow his share. The little man was shivering violently, and had buttoned up his jacket for the first time since fate had pitched them into their jungle hell. Navarr took off his own jacket and gave him that also, but still he hugged the fire, sweating and trembling. By the time the moon came up he was lying back, barely conscious, and, despite the fact that she too was flushed with a slight fever, Lorretta gave him her jacket as well. The sweat was pouring off the little man as he twisted and writhed fitfully, and most of the time Navarr had to hold him down.

Grimly Navarr realised that, unless they were to be again delayed, he would have to use drastic methods for a cure. Leaving Lorretta to watch over Schelde he moved wearily into the darkness of the jungle. He gathered a massive load of dry branches and palm fronds and piled them on top of the restless form. Then he stocked up a great pile of firewood and built up their camp-fire into a blazing furnace that was unbearably hot. He could only hope now that the scorching heat and the weight of the branches and coverings would sweat the fever out of the Belgian's weakened body.

Lorretta had watched him work. She was holding Schelde down by the shoulders, her face was running with sweat from the heat of the fire. The flames cast wavering shadows over her glistening skin, her blue eyes seemed to have sunk much deeper into her face, and she looked terribly tired. The tangled rat's tails of her gold-streaked, auburn hair hung listlessly over her shoulders.

Navarr finished building up the fire and came back to her side. Schelde was beginning to twist again, and he took on the job of holding the little man down. There was a kind of desperate strength in the fevered movements and it was all he could do to hold on and prevent Schelde from kicking aside the jackets and palm fronds that covered him. Lorretta repeatedly wet the sick man's cracked lips with little trickles of water from the can, but Schelde's struggles only grew more frantic. Finally he kicked his legs and threw his coverings aside. Lorretta replaced them and then held him down by the knees. It took all the strength that she and Navarr possessed between them to hold the sweating man still.

The fire flared higher, and the heat became a torture. Now that he had given Schelde his jacket Navarr was again stripped to the waist and the scorching blaze gave a red-bronze glow to his skin. He felt as though he were being roasted alive. Lorretta, who had only her thin blouse, suffered the same torment. The man between them jerked convulsively and moaned aloud.

'Will — will he live, Steve?' Lorretta had to moisten her lips several times with her tongue before she could speak.

Navarr said hoarsely: 'He'll sweat it out. He'll be all right. A bit weak, but all right.'

She looked down at the round dumpy face, running with oily rivulets of sweat. The glasses had fallen off, and the eyes were closed. 'He's bad,' she said. She had to tense to restrain another feverish twist of his body. 'If — if he dies it'll be just the two of us, Steve.' She looked up and her eyes were wide and afraid. 'Who'll be next, Steve? Who'll be next?'

Navarr glared at her. 'Nobody's going to be next, not even Schelde. We're all getting out — even if I have to carry the two of you.'

The harshness of his tone seemed to stun her for a moment. Then she gasped wearily: 'Sure, Steve, he'll live.' A vague smile moved her dried lips. 'Damn it, you bastard! You wouldn't let him die.'

Navarr grinned and then they had to fight to hold down Schelde as he struggled again.

The night crawled on. The moon came out to infiltrate in pale glimmers of light through the trees overhead. The rustlings from the jungle never ceased. Branches moved and leaves stirred from the passage of nocturnal wanderers which they never saw. Jungle rats squeaked in the undergrowth, and unseen lizards scuttled with little scuffling noises across the ground. The jackals for once were silent, but somewhere in the distant forest an elephant was trumpeting its weird shrieking call. The sound froze both Lorretta and Navarr until the latter realised what it was.

Several times Navarr had to release his grip on Schelde in order to rebuild the fire. The giant blaze was like a splash of light in the blackness of the jungle, lighting up the sweating faces of patient and nurses. As the night drew on the mosquitoes found them and transformed the misery of their position into sheer hell, they nipped and stung, drawing little pin points of blood from every area of exposed flesh. Navarr cursed, and did his best to keep them away from the sick man's face. Lorretta suffered in silence.

The mosquitoes brought with them a new fear that troubled Navarr's mind. He was remembering Schelde's gloomy prophecy when the storm had raged about their cave; that the downpour was a forerunner of the monsoon. The arrival of the mosquito swarms seemed to confirm his fears, and Navarr knew that unless they got out before the rainy season started then they would stay there to rot. Their chances of surviving in a jungle ceaselessly battered by deluge after deluge of sheeting rain, the earth slippery with mud, and the air infested with malaria-carrying mosquitoes, were nil.

Another fit of twisting from Schelde drove Navarr's fears from his mind. It was all he could do to hold the man down. The little Belgian was again moaning and his head rolled constantly from one side to the other. Several times he arched his body and hurled some of his coverings off, but each time either Navarr or Lorretta put them back. They were both feeling exhausted by the strain, for they couldn't leave the sick man for a moment. They could only hold him down beneath the heavy covering of branches and hope that he would sweat the fever out by morning.

Midnight came and passed and the early hours of the morning began to drag by. The moon was high and threw vague shadows around the perimeter of their camp. The mosquitoes still harassed them and they kept the fire blazing fiercely. Schelde reached the peak of his fever and writhed and struggled in their grip. As fast as they wiped his forehead fresh sweat would break out and run down his face. His cracked lips moaned continually.

Another hour or two passed before Schelde's struggling died to an occasional twist or turn, and the weight of his nurses was enough to hold him down as they leaned on him. Lorretta managed to spill some more water between his lips, then both she and Navarr took a mouthful to moisten their throats. They returned to watch over their now spent patient, and Navarr again rebuilt the fire.

For another hour they watched over the little Belgian, but the fever's grip was broken. He lay as still as death, his face white and shining, but he no longer moaned or fought and twisted beneath his coverings.

Navarr said wearily: 'Well, that's that! He'll be as weak as a kitten for a few days, but he'll live. We'll just have to help him along.'

'He ought to rest,' she faltered. 'He needs a day or two to regain his strength.'

'A day or two might make all the

difference on Nakai. Besides, there's another thing.' He told her his fears that the monsoon might set in a week or two early and catch them at any time.

She was too weary to react at all to their new danger. She said simply: 'All right, we'll help him along.'

Navarr smiled, and then looked at Schelde who was at last sleeping quietly. He rebuilt the fire beside the man then turned back to Lorretta. 'There's an hour or two of the night left. Let's get some sleep. He'll be okay now.'

She nodded, and he seated himself with his back to a tree a few yards from the fire. She sat down beside him and gratefully leaned in the circle of his arm. He pulled her over and rested her on his chest with her head in the hollow of his neck. His arms locked around her and she closed her hands over his. He held her for a long time, humbled by the touch of her hair where it spilled over his bare shoulder. When finally he kissed her cheek with a tender brushing of his lips she was fast asleep.

16

Two Alone

There was still an hour to go before dawn when Schelde awoke. He was weak, terribly weak, and it took him a long time to remember where he was. The moon was no longer high, and it was pitch dark beyond the pool of light from the blazing fire beside him. The heat was unbearable and seemed to be scorching the skin from his face. He tried to move his head away and then realised how weak he really was. There was neither strength nor will in his body. He felt wet and realised that he was drenched with sweat. Something weighed him down and it took him several moments to recognise the shadowy mound piled over him as a covering of branches and palm fronds. He was painfully thirsty.

He lay there like a limp mass of jelly, and wet his cracked lips with his tongue.

His mouth was dry and he was unable to fetch any saliva into his throat. He wondered if he had been left for dead. The thought tormented him and finally he made a great effort to turn his head. He saw the water bag, the blue canvas holdall with the air company's insignia. It was just out of his reach, and the sight was like a spur to his raging thirst. He forced his eyes away and looked beyond it. He could just make out two misty shapes, their outlines blurred and their features indistinguishable. He thought that they must be Lorretta and Navarr. He wished that he could see properly and wondered where his glasses were.

Ten minutes passed before he again moved his head, and he felt the sharp jab as his spectacles poked into his neck. Weakly he moved one hand up to find them; then he had to pause again before he could push them on to his eyes. They lay there without lodging properly behind his ears and it took him several more minutes to gain the energy to adjust them.

He could see Lorretta and Navarr

clearly now. The girl was in Navarr's arms, her head lolling back on his shoulder. A tree trunk supported the pair of them. Navarr's head had fallen forward and his bearded lips rested against the soft flesh of the girl's throat as though he had dozed off in the very act of kissing her.

Schelde began to move weakly. It took him a long time to pull the small automatic from his pocket. He had never returned it to Navarr after pulling it from Ruth Ballard's dead hand, and the Englishman had been so obsessed in the struggle for survival that he had never noticed. All day Schelde had expected Navarr to demand the weapon, but Navarr had evidently forgotten it completely. Schelde glanced across at the sleeping pair and decided that it would have to be now — now while they were exhausted and unsuspecting.

His duty was clear, but Schelde hesitated. His thoughts went back a long way; long before he had started living a part as Wilhem Schelde. His real name was Kalin Valachia and he had been born in Rumania. He had been in Voron's organisation for a long time.

Always he had hated it, but he was a man who had been ensnared by a chain of events. He had escaped to Belgium during the war, and had later become naturalised. Then one day Voron had appeared, demanding a small service in return for the continued health of the family and friends he had left behind in Bucharest.

Schelde had more than ordinary love for the parents he had left behind. Leaving them had almost broken his heart. So to protect them he obeyed. That first service was a simple matter of driving a car. Other services followed, until eventually a man died as a result of them.

Voron demanded larger favours once that first death had given him a blackmail hold, and soon he began to realise that this particular dupe reacted more favourably when his parents were threatened. He began to see the possibilities, and finally Schelde was promoted from chauffeur to executioner. The first man he eliminated had been shot with a silenced pistol in a darkened alley in Antwerp. The man had been a stranger, a mere name and description issued to him by Voron. It had not been an easy thing to do, but it was easier than the thought of his ailing parents dying or imprisoned. And so it had gone on. After that first man there was another, and then a third.

Somehow Voron had fixed him up with a job that allowed him to travel, arranging export orders for Brestanile Automobiles. How it was arranged was another mystery. Schelde merely did as he was told, he had reached the stage where his weak will had turned to blind obedience and he simply followed his instructions to the letter. He never asked questions. He was, in fact, the perfect tool. He had quelled his own personality because that way he could still his conscience, too. He just did as he was ordered, carrying messages under the cover of his respectable job. Once in a while there would be another man or woman who had to be eliminated: a filthy looking apache in the back streets of Paris; a baby-faced American in Madrid; a hard-eyed harlot in a seedy bedroom in Tel Aviv.

On the surface Schelde was just a fumbling little car-exporter; an act he adopted to hide his identity as a hardened killer for a vicious organisation. But beneath that another shell developed. He drew a parallel between his own motives and actions, and those of the thousands of God-fearing men who had killed during wartime to protect their families and their homes. He convinced himself that he was no more a murderer than they were, for in actual fact he was doing no more than they had done; namely, carrying out orders to kill his country's enemies and protect his own. And in that way he sometimes gained relief from his tortured conscience.

Through the years he had become one of Voron's most trusted agents, for Voron knew full well the strength of the chains that held the little man's loyalty. Voron had studied his man, and he assessed his mental attitude with diabolical skill. As long as he was in a position to threaten the elderly Valachia couple in Bucharest, so he could control their son Kalin, like a puppet on a string.

So it went on, until finally Voron had needed a reserve man he could trust on the islands of Nakai. His present project was too big to risk failure by not having a good man ready to deal with any unseen emergencies. So, indirectly, he had arranged for Schelde to be sent there by his firm, the ways and means of the arrangements being again a mystery to the man concerned. Schelde had concluded his official business, and had then waited at his hotel until a telephone call had sent him racing to the airport where Larrieux had been cornered. There he was told nothing except that the man had to be eliminated before he could talk. That was all.

The shooting down of the airliner was something that he had not expected, and it had set him an almost impossible task. He knew that if any of them survived with him and passed on the French agent's story in time to foil Voron's plans, then he, too, would die and with him the loved ones he had killed so many times to save.

At first it had been easy. The two airmen, and then Asaka, whom he had killed with a judo blow, were just another three enemies in his endless war. It had been harder to bring himself to kill Dorapho, and by the time he came to start the landslide that had killed Rex and Ruth Ballard he realised that they were no longer nameless strangers; they had become friends, allies, and with the little woman he had saved from the crash, it was more than that. For the first time another human being had penetrated the shield around his heart. He had come to love Ruth Ballard, and to like and respect his friends.

He knew then that he hated Voron for what the man had made of him, but there was nothing he could do. He had waited several minutes in that raging storm before realising that it was too late to stop now. If he stopped, then every murder that stained his hands would have been a death in vain. He hesitated and then gave the boulder that started the slide a hard push. Then he lurched away, clapping his hands to his ears as if that might shut the deed out. It hadn't, and Ruth Ballard's scream had torn open his heart. In that moment the little man had wished himself dead, and longed for his punishment in hell.

The fire began to grow dimmer as Schelde's thoughts wandered; and finally the fact that he was beginning to feel cold brought his mind back to the present. He glanced across to Navarr, and remembered how the tall man had automatically trained himself to wake when it grew cold, for he had watched him closely the night before. If he was going to act before Navarr awoke, he would have to act now.

He pushed the branches and jackets aside with a sharp, determined effort, and half rolled towards the water bag. It was unzipped and he reached one hand inside and scooped a handful of water to his mouth. His throat was still dry and rasping and his tongue was like a limp strip of blanket in his mouth. He had to have a drink. He moistened his throat, and somehow it instilled him with a new energy. Shakily he pulled himself to his knees and then began to shiver with cold. His teeth chattered as he straightened up. He swayed weakly and wondered how long it would take him to die once he had finished his task. He hoped that it wouldn't take long. He wanted to die now.

He took a stumbling step forward and raised the revolver. He pointed it at Navarr's head but couldn't steady his hand, it was trembling so. Sweat broke out on his brow and he felt his knees begin to buckle under him. He took another step, until he was holding the gun only a yard away from Navarr's head. His hand still wavered, but he felt that from there he couldn't miss. He made a last attempt to steady the gun, which seemed to have become so heavy, before firing.

In that moment Lorretta opened her eyes. For a moment she stared at the swaying man — then she screamed. The sound seemed to stun the half-conscious agent and his mouth gaped stupidly. Then Lorretta threw herself to one side, dragging Navarr with her. In the same moment Schelde fired.

Navarr was jerked awake by the scream, and felt Lorretta dragging him aside seconds before the bullet traced a streak of agony across his arm. The bullet thudded into the tree in the same moment that his shoulders slipped away from it and he fell to the ground. The pain snapped him wide awake, and he saw Schelde staggering as he attempted to aim the gun again. Desperately Navarr kept on rolling, dragging Lorretta with him. Schelde fired again — then they both crashed into the undergrowth and were out of the circle of firelight. Within seconds Navarr was stumbling to his knees and dragging the girl deeper into the blackness, as Schelde sent another frantic shot after them.

Unseen branches and vines beat at them as they continued their headlong flight through the darkness. Then, abruptly, Navarr jerked to a halt and Lorretta stumbled into him. She clung to him desperately, and he peered over her shoulder into the silent jungle. There was no sign of Schelde. He began to relax then for it was obvious that Schelde was in no condition to pursue them into the jungle. He enveloped Lorretta's trembling body in his arms, and heard her sob with her face pressed to his chest. He stood there breathing heavily and felt the slight wound across his arm begin to burn viciously. He had to grit his teeth against the pain and he felt a warm trickle course down his naked arm.

It was several minutes before the realisation that he had been wounded made Lorretta steady her shaking nerves. She felt the stickiness of blood on her hand and uttered a sharp exclamation of alarm.

Navarr said quickly: 'It's okay, just a graze. Smarting like hell, but it's not serious.' He still held her tight and sensed that she was looking up into his face, although when he looked down he couldn't even see her. He said grimly: 'Let's move back slowly. Schelde may have collapsed after that shooting. He looked more dead than alive. And he has the water.'

She said nothing, clinging tightly to

his arm as he moved cautiously back the way they had come. He felt his way blindly with one hand, his injured arm still around her. Schelde's actions had clearly been a last-minute do-or-die effort, and it was quite possible that he had collapsed after they had got away. It was also possible that he had enough strength to lie in wait for them in case they tried to retrieve the water, so they had to move silently. Navarr would have preferred to leave Lorretta out of harm's way, but he doubted if he could ever find her again in the jungle night, without attracting Schelde's attention as well.

After a few minutes they saw the glow of the fire through the trees, and they stepped as lightly and silently as possible as they closed in. The foliage rustled around them, but the jungle was full of rustlings, and Navarr hoped that theirs were no louder than the rest.

At last they were able to see into the firelit clearing. It was deserted. Schelde was gone, and so was the precious water bag. Gone, too, were both their jackets and their bow.

Navarr backed up into the darkness of the jungle and gently pulled Lorretta with him. They turned and felt their way cautiously along until they were well out of sight of the fire. Their eyes were used to the blackness now, and Navarr could just make out Lorretta's profile as she looked up at him.

He said grimly: 'Schelde must have recovered enough to know what he was doing. He's left the fire because he knows damn well that he's too weak to do anything if I try to surprise him. He's got the water and our coats, he has the sense to know that in his condition he'll have to keep himself warm. He'll probably die, anyway.'

'What about us, Steve? What are our chances now?'

'We'll go on till we drop,' he said simply. 'We could never find Schelde in the jungle and retrieve that water, so we just have to go on. We'll last a couple of days. Either we'll find a village or hit the river in that time — or we won't.'

There was nothing they could do then except rest in the blackness of the jungle, waiting for the dawn. When it came, they moved determinedly eastwards once more, neither knowing, nor caring, whether Schelde was alive or dead.

Navarr still had his watch on his wrist and they kept to a set routine of marching for an hour and then taking a ten-minute rest. The sun climbed higher as the day wore on, and as it climbed so their strength faded. Navarr was now bare to the waist, and if the tree-tops had not shut out the direct heat he would have been badly burnt. He kept one arm fast about Lorretta's shoulders as they struggled on.

The world became a misty nightmare of endless green foliage and stifling heat. They fell over many times, and had to lie panting before they found the energy to go on. Their bodies became slippery with sweat and their throats dry. Thirst became a torment, and Lorretta's cracked lips finally split open. Before nightfall Navarr was in the same state.

Their movements became automatic, and when one slipped, the other strove to stay firm. They hardly spoke a word throughout the long day, for neither had the strength to spare for talking. Without water or the means to hunt they knew that their time was limited. As it was getting dusk they finally collapsed and Navarr had no strength left to build a fire. They were in a small clearing where it was possible to lie full length, and they lay like lovers in one another's arms. Night closed in, and the nocturnal sounds of the jungle began again. Neither of them heard or cared. They lay close, and if it was decreed that they should die in the night then they would die together.

★ ★ ★

A mile behind them Schelde also lay half-dead in the jungle night. The little man had gathered up the water bag and the two jackets and the bow after Navarr and Lorretta had fled into the jungle, and had staggered away in the opposite direction. He had made a hundred yards before collapsing and he had tried to pull the jackets over his shivering limbs. He had failed, but he was hardly aware of the fact then, for he instantly passed out.

He had recovered a few hours after dawn, still pitifully weak and with a raging thirst. The water bag was beside him and he drank deeply, reviving a little as the tepid water ran down his throat.

After a while, he fumbled in his pocket and drew out a piece of the roast meat they had cut from the tiger's haunch. It was charred, stringy, and tasteless, he forced some into his mouth but instantly brought it up. Determinedly, he forced himself to eat on until he had managed to keep some down. Then he staggered to his feet, jettisoned everything except one other piece of meat, the water, and the automatic, and stumbled out of the clearing.

He knew that Navarr would keep heading due east, so it was quite easy to pick up his trail. He moved like an automaton all day, falling and getting up again every few minutes. He drank often and, despite his weakness from the fever, the fact that he had meat and drink made him almost as capable as Navarr. He kept going, and nightfall found him only a mile or so behind the other two. Then he collapsed into an exhausted coma in the blackness, keeping one hand on the water bag and one on the automatic. His last thought was that he would have to catch up with Navarr soon, catch him and kill him. Soon it would be too late. Soon he would be dead himself.

17

More Than a Man

The heat of the sun woke Navarr several hours after dawn the following morning. He felt as weak as death, and for a long time he could do nothing but stare into the haggard face a few inches from his own. Lorretta's eyes were closed and her cheeks were hollow. She was lying on his left arm and his right was around her waist. She was holding him close, and there was something deeply peaceful in her breathing. If he had had the strength he would not have had the heart to disturb her, and he let her sleep on in his arms. Flies were crawling around the black scab on his injured arm, but he did not move. He let her sleep until finally he allowed his mouth to touch her split lips in the ghost of a kiss.

Her eyes blinked open, blue and uncertain behind the wavering lashes.

She swallowed several times before she could get enough moisture into her mouth to speak.

'Hello, Steve.'

He kissed her again. 'The last day,' he said. 'Today is the day we get out.' He tried to sound cheerful, as if he didn't know that it would have to be the last day because they would be too weak to move tomorrow.

She lay still in his arms. 'Promise me, Steve — promise me you'll hold me like this tonight?'

He smiled, mostly with his eyes. 'That will hardly be proper, we're going to sleep in a bed tonight. But I'll hold you.'

She trembled as his lips touched hers for the third time.

'All right, Steve. I'm ready.'

He stood up, slowly, like a man reaching for a mountain top at an incredibly high altitude where there was barely a breath of oxygen. For a moment he swayed, then he reached down and drew her up beside him. She leaned against his naked chest and her legs all but buckled beneath her. Then they started to move again, east, always east.

It became easier once they had started. Getting moving was always the major effort, once they began to walk their own momentum carried them on. They relapsed into that blessed state where they were hardly aware of what they were doing, not seeing their surroundings, just stumbling on.

By noon Navarr was supporting practically all of Lorretta's weight as she leaned against him. Finally he lowered her into a comparatively cool patch of shade, and sank down beside her. His tongue was beginning to swell and he wondered how long it would take for it to choke him. He knew that Lorretta could be no better off, and steeled himself for the hours to come.

He waited until the sun was on the decline and then lifted her up. She leaned against him as they moved off, and he had to half drag her along. Every time they fell it took him an age to regain his feet and haul her up beside him. The blazing sun showed them no mercy. Their mouths were full of nothing but hot, dry air, their throats were choked by the swelling leather of their tongues.

They fell for what seemed the thousandth time, and again Navarr fought his way slowly to his feet. There was a smooth-stemmed tree before him and he used it to pull himself painfully upright. There was something familiar about the tree, but not until he saw the green-skinned fruit did memory register. It was the same type of tree that Chang Lee had pointed out to him when they first searched for water. The green fruits were limes.

With fumbling fingers Navarr tore the fruit down and dug at the rind with his broken nails. Lorretta sprawled face down beside him and he turned her over and forced her to eat. The acid-tasting juice stung like fire against their cracked lips, but it was moisture to allay their raging thirst, a gift from the gods that would enable them to last a little longer. Navarr gathered what few fruits were left on the tree and stuffed them into his pockets. Then he got Lorretta to her feet again, and once more they moved on.

Although slightly refreshed they were still terribly weak, and Navarr's mind began to wander as they stumbled forwards. He moved in a dream and kept seeing the faces of his past companions smiling at him, Schelde was among them, shooting at things with his little gun. He hardly knew what he was doing and decided that the heat was driving him crazy.

They tripped and sprawled headlong into the undergrowth, and when Navarr pulled Lorretta up she croaked something about her foot. He looked down stupidly and saw that her left foot was bare. It was bleeding and red stains splashed the grass where she stood. He asked her where she had lost her shoe.

'In the jungle,' she said carefully, and then giggled.

'I'll go back and look for it,' he said.

'No, it's no use, Steve.' Her senses seemed to clarify and she looked up at him. 'I lost it a long time ago. I don't know how long.' Her blue eyes became suddenly clearer and she said: 'Leave me, Steve! You'll never make it with me.'

336

He stared, the idea was unthinkable. 'We'll both make it,' he said. 'Besides, I made a promise to you.'

'I was being selfish.' Her voice was horribly cracked. 'I — I had forgotten about Nakai.'

He tried to pull her forwards, but she simply collapsed. She lay without moving, and he knelt beside her, burrowed his hands beneath her, lifted her up, and staggered drunkenly on.

He was aware of only one thing now. He had to keep going, and he had to take Lorretta with him. He was sliding his feet grimly forwards, one at a time. First the left foot — then the right. Branches kept clutching at Lorretta's dangling head and legs, but there was nothing he could do to avoid them. First the left foot — then the right. His back was breaking, his legs wanted to buckle, leaves and foliage slapped him in the face. His mind was hazy — first the left foot, then the right. Lorretta lay like death in his arms. First the left foot — then the — He fell heavily, crashing on top of her, then rolling helplessly away.

It was pitch-dark when he revived enough to crawl towards her. He felt the outline of her body, and weakly croaked her name. There was no answer, and only her breathing told him that she was alive. His eyes became accustomed to the dark and he saw a clump of mossy boulders nearby. Slowly he dragged her into the shelter of the rocks and tried to make her eat some more of the green limes.

The bitter sting of the raw fruit revived her a little, and afterwards she said slowly:

'Steve, you promised.'

He let her come into his arms and they slept together, blanketed by the jungle tree-tops and the night sky.

★ ★ ★

Schelde spent the night only a quarter of a mile behind them. He had finished the last of the water and discarded the blue holdall, and after eating what little he could stomach of the meat he carried, he had thrown the rest away. He had only the gun now, the gun he needed to kill Steve Navarr.

He dreamed while he slept. Dreamed of a small stone farmhouse, set in rich, rolling pastureland amid a background of dark, wooded mountains. Below the farmhouse, fields of yellow grain waved in the bright sunlight. An old woman waited in the crude doorway, her hair white and wispy above a care-lined face. She was watching an old man coming up the hill. The couple met, smiled fondly, and disappeared into the house.

It was a simple dream, and it soon faded, faded to a drab street in Bucharest where the old couple now lived, faded into a nightmare where silent men dragged them into the darkened street, while the razor-nosed features of Voron hovered in the background. Blood was spilled, and Voron was laughing.

Schelde awoke, screaming. He lay face down on the damp earth and slowly brought his trembling nerves under control. The dream would stop. He had stopped it before, and he could stop it again. He could avoid failure by killing the last two survivors who could tell Pierre Larrieux's story.

The little man would have preferred to die rather than to carry on killing those who had befriended him. But that would not help his parents. If Navarr lived to tell his story, then Voron would know he had failed. Suicide was useless. There was no way out.

Schelde's mind had been schooled exactly the way Voron had intended.

★ ★ ★

It seemed to Navarr that he had barely closed his eyes before the sun was again hot on his naked back. He lay for a long time, eyes closed, unmoving, aware only of the burning heat on his shoulders. He could feel the vague movements of life in the unconscious body in his arms, and he thought suddenly that this was a good way to die. He no longer had the strength to get up. He was finished, but at least the woman he loved was in his arms. He wanted to open his eyes and look at her, but he couldn't. Instead he

340

contented himself with the feel of her as she lay against him. He tried to tighten his arms but he failed there as well, they just lay limp around her.

Perhaps an hour passed, perhaps more. A lone vulture watched from above, knowing they were still alive, but waiting his time. A bright-eyed lizard eyed them curiously and then scurried away. Navarr felt the heat flaying his skin. The heat reminded him of something but he did not know what it was. He did not even care. Then suddenly he remembered. Heat was what would destroy Nakai, the fantastic blazing heat as Voron detonated his atom bomb over the great air base. He saw again the fiendish tower of smoke rising and spreading from the doomed islands, saw again the ghastly slaughter that would accompany the holocaust. Slowly he stirred into movement.

It took him an age to reach his knees and he stayed there and leaned against the rocks. He blinked several times before he could clear his vision, then he looked down at the seemingly lifeless girl beside him. He shook her gently. She did not stir and he shook her again. He had to shake her brutally before she opened her eyes.

'Last day,' he managed to say weakly. He seemed to remember saying that before, but couldn't remember when. He added: 'It's not far now.' He fumbled in his pockets for the last two limes. He half peeled one and made the effort of helping her to sit up and eat. Somehow they got the last of the fruit down.

It took another tremendous effort to get started, then somehow they were lurching on again. Navarr had Lorretta's arm over his shoulders and half-carried her. Soon the heat made them light-headed once more.

Navarr's mind drifted back into the world of fantasy. Their dead friends were there again, staring and willing him on. Kelley's boyish face was tense, Connors grim, Dorapho's pock-marked cheeks were still villainous. Rex laughed and called him 'hardcase'. They all began to whirl about him, like disembodied ghosts in his mind. Kelley — Connors — Chang Lee — Asaka. Kelley again. Rex — Schelde shooting his absurd gun.

Ruth calling him Howard.

He realised that he was going crazy, that the sun was twisting his brain. He was alone except for the girl who clung to him, and the faces of his dead companions dissolved into ordinary palm fronds or jasmine flowers.

Lorretta finally fell forwards again, dragging him with her. He stayed on his hands and knees as she rolled away and stared at her dumbly. Fresh blood streaked her cut foot, and he wondered why she was so limp and doll-like. She stared at him and her lips moved grotesquely:

'Go on, Steve! You — you've got to leave me.'

'Don't be — bloody fool.' He wished that he hadn't used the swear word, and tried to apologise, but nothing else would come.

He got up without knowing how, and somehow he pulled her up beside him. He held her steady for a moment, and stared at her. Her blouse had torn wholly open, and there was a steady stream of sweat running into the deep valley between her glistening breasts. He watched it stupidly and then looked into her face. There was no expression in her eyes, no embarrassment. They were too close now ever to be embarrassed by each other. He pulled her close and she fell against him. He kissed her split lips.

'Good girl,' he said. 'We'll make it.'

He stumbled forwards and pulled her with him.

The sun was very high now, and the heat seemed to lay around them in ever tightening coils. It was difficult to breathe the stifling air and their mouths were dried up and tasteless. The ache in Navarr's skull developed into a fury of pain. He moved blindly forward until they again fell face down in the undergrowth.

Navarr wondered how many times he had fallen down and staggered up. It must have been hundreds. He told himself defiantly that what he had done so many times before he could do again. He began the long, tiring effort to get to his knees, gasping and fighting the heat that held him down like a giant blanket. He got to his knees, and looked for Lorretta. She looked doll-like again, sprawled on her back with her arms outstretched, and her eyes closed. She breathed slowly, long, deep breaths that were almost too much trouble to draw. He knew she couldn't get up this time and he realised that he would have to carry her. He got his hands beneath her shoulders and knees, then, with a slow surge of effort, he lifted her in his arms and rose to his feet. He almost blacked out and he closed his eyes until the nausea of dizziness had passed, then he moved slowly on. The sun was directly overhead, but still he kept going, something told him that he would never get up if he once stopped to rest.

Steve Navarr became more than a man during the next desperate hours. He staggered on with Lorretta in his arms; a physical wreck propelled only by the raw instinct for survival. Long after his legs should have buckled beneath him, he kept going on his heart alone. Where another man would have laid down and died, Navarr kept blindly on. He was almost beyond feeling now, numbed by the heat and the burning sun. He had just one thought: to keep on moving.

He thought of Voron and Nakai, of the bright silver bomber that would disintegrate into the fiery horror of an atomic explosion one bright peaceful morning. He thought of the thousands who would die, and of his companions who had already died in trying to prevent the disaster. But most of all he thought of the limp form in his arms, the dying girl he could not leave behind. He *had* to survive.

His thoughts all merged into that one guiding phrase — He had to survive. The dying face of Pierre Larrieux swam into his mind like a faint spirit in a dense mist. The man croaked at him feverishly: 'One of you must survive.' 'One of you must survive.' And then suddenly Kelley, Connors, Dorapho and the rest were there again, dead visions from the past drifting in the vaporous haze of his mind. Their voices reached him from far away, eerie, distorted: 'One of you must survive.' *'One of you must survive.'*

And now he was the only one left.

He fell again, crashing heavily on top of the girl, hearing her moan through cracked lips with the impact of his weight. The voices in his brain spurred him like verbal lashes, and with a superhuman effort he rose once more to his feet. Once more he staggered on with the girl in his arms.

He knew nothing now of the springy branches that whipped them both, knew nothing of the chattering parrots that called down as he passed. The undergrowth caught at his legs and tore the flesh through the frayed tatters of his trousers, but he felt nothing. He pushed his way through the never-ending barrier without ever seeing it. Even the blazing sun seemed vague and distant, like something from another world. In his world there was nothing — nothing but the dull need to go on.

The jungle giants grew gradually taller but he never noticed as he stumbled on. They towered immensely high above him and the ground where he walked became densely shadowed, almost as dark as night. It made no impression on him, however, as he fought his grim battle alone. Somewhere not too far away an elephant trumpeted shrilly and somewhere beyond another answered faintly. The sounds meant nothing to him. The wet, cloying heat was about the only thing strong enough now to penetrate his numbed brain, and even that was just a dim, almost unreal, discomfort.

He fell again. His face was buried in a rotting mess of wet leaves, and it was all he could do to turn his face to prevent himself from suffocating. He felt Lorretta stir beneath him, and heard her moan anew, but there was nothing he could do. He was finished. He had determined to go on until he dropped — and now he had dropped for the last time. He stared at the dank brown leaves just before his eyes, and wondered if he could turn his body so that he could lie beside the girl instead of across her. He began to try, dragging himself round in the wet undergrowth. It took him a long while, but he finally managed it. Her face was a death's mask, and he kissed the split lips for what he thought must be the last time. The touch made her open her eyes. She stared up, then her lips moved.

'Look,' she said. That was all, but despite the hoarse rasping tone there was a gleam that was almost hope in her eyes.

He turned his head slowly and focused his bleary eyes. Something swam before them and then slowly clarified. It was the stump of a cut-down tree. He gaped at it stupidly as though the thing were a mirage and then he saw other stumps beyond it. Slowly it sank into his dazed brain that they were in a teak forest. Somewhere near there had to be a logging camp.

He looked down at Lorretta and a new determination seeped through his seemingly boneless limbs. They couldn't give up now! Not now that they were so near. As if to shore up his courage another elephant trumpeted, not too far away. He realised that elephants were used for haulage in the teak forests, and that where the elephants were he would find men.

The realisation seemed to sink into her mind, too, for she found a last dim vestige of strength and struggled up to a sitting position beside him. He saw her smile and held her in his arms, each supporting the other.

'Nearly there,' he said. And then he kissed her again. 'One more try,' he croaked. 'Good girl!'

She smiled the cracked smile again, and her sunken eyes stirred with a faint light. Then, abruptly, her eyes fixed on a spot just beyond his shoulder and her tired body stiffened in his hands. The dead expression on her face might have been one of despair or horror if only she had not long since lost the will to react to anything. Her blue eyes glazed over dully, and slowly Navarr turned his head.

Five yards away a swaying, hooded head reared out of the undergrowth. Black eyes gleamed above the flared hood and the thick trailing neck vanished into the vegetation. Navarr recognised the hissing monster as a giant hamadryad, the deadly King Cobra of Burma. He shut his eyes hopelessly as the hissing head swayed nearer.

A shot made him open them again, the sharp report of a small-calibred automatic. He saw the hooded head knocked aside as the bullet smacked into it, and then the writhing body flailed into the undergrowth. The great snake squirmed for several minutes and then lay still. Slowly Navarr looked up, and his heart sank again. Supporting himself on a tree barely a dozen feet away was Schelde. An incredibly ravaged shadow of the Schelde they had known, but still Schelde. He had shot the King Cobra from a range of just three feet and now the gun in his hand pointed steadily at Navarr.

18

In the Balance

Navarr stared dumbly at the little Belgian, hardly able to believe his eyes. He had given Schelde up for dead and now the man stood there like a ghost, more dead than alive, the rags of his clothing hanging in tatters on his skeleton frame. He had lost his hat and the front of his skull was red and blistered below the hairline. It was a miracle that he had not suffered sunstroke. The tiny gun looked large in his skinny fingers, and it was clear that he had only to let go of his supporting tree to collapse.

It was Navarr who spoke first. He glanced from the gun to the dead cobra and asked huskily: 'Why did you bother? He would have saved you the trouble.'

Schelde gaped at him, and his mouth worked half a dozen times before he could speak. Navarr guessed that his tongue was badly swollen. Finally he croaked: 'I do not know. I see the snake and — and shoot. There was no time to think.'

Navarr got out weakly: 'We saved your life, remember?' He didn't expect it to do any good.

'Yes, yes — I remember.' He swayed unsteadily. 'I have been remembering for three days. You make it hard. All the others I could kill, but you have to save my life. Even the Greek's death was my doing. I kicked his feet from under him in the river.'

'Bloody murderer!'

'No, I kill only because I have to.'

'Bloody murderer!' Navarr croaked again.

Schelde went on as if he had not heard. 'Voron — Voron sent me to kill the Frenchman. Then, after we were shot down, I knew I had to kill you all. If anyone escaped I knew he would kill me for allowing it. Besides, he would kill my parents. You see. I am not Belgian, I was born in Rumania. Voron will — will kill my people if I do not follow his orders.

He is that kind of — *bastard*.'

The word bastard had a particularly venomous quality the way Schelde used it, he made it a symbol of everything vile and evil that could be found in a human being.

Lorretta spoke, raspingly. 'You swine! You even killed Ruth. You saved her life — helped her — then murdered her. It was all an act.'

The barb wrung a twisted cry from the emaciated wreck by the tree.

'No! No! I was very — very fond of Mrs. Ballard. But I had no choice. You do not understand. You have to be born on the wrong side of the world before you can ever understand. I have killed many times — but only to protect my parents.'

Navarr believed the man then. It was not hard to believe that a dumpy, spectacled, and unromantic little character like Schelde had an overpowering affection for his parents. It was not hard, either, to believe that Voron was the kind of ruthless communist who would take such diabolical advantage of the situation.

Navarr felt almost sorry for Schelde in that moment.

Schelde croaked on: 'It would take years to explain how an agent like Voron turns a man into a killer. But — but now, in these last hours, I have seen a way out. If Voron learns that I have survived he will take his vengeance on my parents. He would have them imprisoned — it would mean their death. If he thought I cheated him by suicide he would kill them for that. He warned me once about that. But now I see a way. You, Navarr, you will tell no one I survived?'

'Dead men tell no tales.' There was a faint note of the old cynicism in Navarr's tone.

'No.' Schelde shook his head weakly and sweat streamed down his face. 'No, you will live. But — but you will let everyone believe that I died in the plane crash. No one will know that I survived.'

'I'll see you in hell first.'

A ghastly mask of a smile twisted Schelde's lips.

'You will do it, Navarr. That is why I had to catch you. You will let Voron believe that I died in that plane. You will let him believe it so that he will not victimise my parents, whom I swear before God are innocent. They know nothing of what I have had to do to protect them. You will do this because — because that is the kind of man you are, Navarr.'

Navarr stared dumbly, not knowing what to say. The full meaning of the little man's words had not yet penetrated his aching brain but Schelde was smiling his death's-head grin as if he knew that it only needed time.

The grinning murderer said weakly: 'Remember, Navarr. When you tell your story, I never came out of that burning plane alive. And nobody was murdered — they all died natural deaths. You see, Navarr, this is one time I cannot kill. I know you too well, once you have saved my life. I killed Ruth Ballard and made my conscience into a hell of torment. I have not the will to do it again.'

Navarr watched as the little man lifted the automatic and placed the snub barrel behind his own ear.

'Remember,' he said. 'I died in the plane. You are not the man to let Voron take his vengeance upon the innocent.' He had to fight to work his mouth and get out his last croaking words. 'I wish to God I had seen this way out before.'

His finger closed on the trigger and the small-calibre bullet tore his brains out with a savage bark.

Navarr turned his head away as Schelde finished speaking, and crushed Lorretta's face to his chest. For an eternity there was no sound as the echoes of the shot died away into the jungle, then there came a dull crash as the body slipped from the tree and hit the undergrowth. Navarr forced his gaze round and saw the dumpy little form stretched on its side, the head hidden in a clump of ferns. He was glad, he didn't want to see the head.

He turned his face again and contented himself for a moment with holding Lorretta close. He felt that he was beginning to understand something of the character of the man who had called himself Wilhem Schelde, and deep inside he knew that the man was right. He would say nothing of the murders that had dogged their footsteps. There was nothing to be gained by speaking now. A few moments ago he had been sorry for the little man, but now he was dead that sorrow died, too. Schelde had been trapped in a web where he had been forced to kill to save those he loved. Many had done so before him, and many would do so again. The fact that the threat came, not from those he had killed, but from those who made him kill was something that was beyond his control.

Navarr realised that he was glad that Schelde had finally found a way out. Voron had insured against deliberate suicide by warning him that it would not save his parents. Only now Voron himself had supplied him with a perfect cover of accidental death, and Navarr was determined to let it stand. Maybe they owed Schelde nothing, but they had no cause for vengeance on his family either.

Lorretta said suddenly: 'Listen.'

He looked down at her face and stared at her somewhat stupidly. Then the sound reached his ears, it was another elephant trumpeting. He realised anew that they were in a forest of teak, and the cry of the elephant filled him with the hope that there would be a logging camp nearby.

He croaked slowly: 'Let's go, we can't give up now.'

She shook her head slowly, the tangled rat's-tails brushing her dirt-streaked shoulders. 'No, Steve,' her eyes were haggard and her split lips barely moving. 'You go on. You can send somebody back for me. You — you'll make it alone.'

He said nothing, concentrating all his strength and energy in getting to his feet. A short while ago he had considered himself finished, but the hope fed by that trumpeting elephant had untapped some minute and distant source of will-power. For an eternity he seemed to be fighting, making a terrific effort to control his weak limbs; then somehow he was on his feet. He reached down and gripped her arm. She stared up helplessly as he pulled. He had to fight another battle then, one even more demanding than the first. He strained until the jungle spun in dizzy circles around his aching brain. Spearheads of light penetrated his closed eyes and pierced his skull. The pain of it made him want to scream. Lorretta lay limp at his feet, then something of his raw courage, his indomitable defiance, was slowly absorbed into her heart. She began to push herself up, and, miraculously, they were both on their feet.

Navarr knew that despite her grim determination Lorretta would never walk. He swayed as she leaned back on his arm and then made his last fantastic effort. He hooked his other arm behind her knees and with one titanic heave he lifted her up.

He began to move again, one stumbling step at a time. He heard the trumpeting of the elephant once more, and moved blindly towards it, praying that he would not fall, for to fall would mean the end.

'Leave me, Steve!' it was a pitiful croaking appeal, an appeal to him to save his own life. But Navarr ignored it. In his mind he was fighting a personal battle, a battle for the prize of thousands of lives, together with the life and love of the woman in his arms. And Steve Navarr would relinquish neither.

Somehow he remained erect as he made his faltering way through the jungle. A root or a tangle of undergrowth could have spelt the end, but nothing caught at his blistered feet. The jungle that had fought him all the way seemed to have relented in the face of sheer courage and now made no attempt to bring him down. And then abruptly he stepped out on to a path, a narrow cleared track that ran through an area where the giant trees had been felled. He lurched forward drunkenly with the woman in his arms, then a guiding scream from an elephant made him turn to his left. Somehow he got moving again, slithering his feet painfully along the hard packed earth.

He was walking blindly now, his eyes screwed tight against the agonising ache in his brain. His tongue was swelling in his throat, and his mouth gaped open. In the last few yards he had lost his hat, the half-burnt, floppy hat which he had worn so long, and his head was unprotected. Around him the teak giants had been felled, and the sun beamed in concentrated fury on his skull. Fresh blood was running where the black scab had lifted on his wounded arm, but he knew nothing of it as he slid one foot slowly in front of the other. The dead ghosts of his past companions returned again to mark his way, drifting through the pain-filled mists within his brain. He was dead, finished — yet somehow it was just possible to keep moving. Every step should have been his last, but somehow he always made one more. Lorretta was a dead, unmoving weight now, and he was uncertain whether she was still alive. Yet blindly he made another step — another step — and yet another.

How long that last tortured stage of the journey took Navarr never knew. He might have been hours on that narrow track, or he might only have been minutes. He moved on the impulse of his great heart alone, his body was long since finished. He heard the trumpeting of the elephants, many of them, vaguely nearer.

The sound spurred more will power into his frame. Every movement was an agony now; every sinew was stretched to breaking point, every nerve crying for release. Somehow he took another step — another step — yet another step.

A shout stopped him, a startled exclamation in a strange tongue. He faltered. Again the voice, shouting, excited. A second voice answered, strange and jabbering. With an effort he raised his sagging head and unscrewed his aching eyes. He saw two ghosts, two wavering ghosts that danced and swayed through a veil of pain. Two hazy outlines that were like demons in a swirling mist of heat and sweat. Then gradually they became clearer, solidified. They were Burmese; two short, stocky little men in soiled and loose-fitting pants that came down to their knees. Both wore turbans of dirty cloth, and one had a large knife slung over his shoulders by a cord. They were staring with pop eyes and open mouths as if half afraid of what they had found.

Navarr uttered a croaking cry, and stumbled towards them. He covered two lurching steps before crashing forwards. Lorretta fell out of his arms, and he sprawled on top of her. His face hit the hard earth and he passed out.

His last thought was a sense of eternal gratitude because he could still feel the soft contours of Lorretta's body beneath him. At least, they were still together.

19

An Unofficial Thank you

A week had passed, and Lorretta de Valoise and Steve Navarr sat side by side in large comfortable chairs in one of the private rooms in the British Embassy in Rangoon. The intervening time they had spent under careful nursing in a hospital in Mandalay, after being brought out of the jungle by the white manager of the teak logging camp.

Now they were both looking reasonably fit. They still limped slightly from their blisters, and Navarr's arm was neatly bandaged. Only when you looked closely did it become apparent that they were still thin and pale, and that Lorretta's slim legs were scratched and marked beneath her sheer nylons.

At the moment Lorretta was leaning back in her chair, toying with an elegant sherry glass. Her hair was once more a silky, flowing wave, only now it was a natural auburn and it flashed with red lights in the sun's rays that sneaked through the slatted window. She was wearing a simple red print frock to match her hair, and her feet were encased in open-toed sandals, made of soft leather and beautifully decorated. The cracks in her lips had healed, and they were now a moist, cherry red. Her blue eyes were alive again with a slight sparkle.

Beside her Navarr had shaved off his fearsome black beard, and his lean face looked human again. Something of the old cynical smile still remained in his eyes as he looked about him. He was dressed in an open-necked white shirt and grey slacks, the short sleeves of the shirt didn't quite cover the bandage on his right arm.

They were facing the British Consul for Burma, and at the moment he was doing the talking. 'You're both looking quite fit,' he told them. 'I hear that you were more dead than alive when Melford's natives found you near his camp. You were damned lucky to strike that, you know. If you had missed it, you would have had another thirty miles to go before you came out on the Irrawaddy. Still — I suppose what you really want to know is what happened after you passed that report from that young Frenchman on to us?'

Navarr nodded. 'We know very little. As soon as I was able to talk I told the doctor at the hospital, and made him swear to pass it on. He assured me that he had done so, but he knew nothing of what was happening.'

The Consul smiled. 'The way I heard it you croaked it out the second you came to in the hospital, only a few hours after Melford had rushed you both there by jeep. The doctors thought you had sunstroke, but somehow you convinced them. Thank God you did!'

'It's been stopped then?'

'Yes, we passed your story straight on to the American Embassy, and they informed the security people on Nakai within a matter of minutes, as soon as they could get a coded message through. The people there had worked with this fellow Larrieux and they acted on it as gospel. They grounded all planes and searched the lot. They found a little suitcase, no bigger than an over-night case, hidden aboard a transport plane. When they opened it the bomb was inside. They dismantled it, and once they were safe they went all out to rope in the three men you were able to describe. The man Voron they already had under close observation, but he swallowed a capsule of poison seconds before they reached him. He died an instant death. The other two, Kang and Calostro, were cornered in their dug-out on the mountainside. The whole mountain was searched for that remote control equipment, and the radio and they were with it. They tried to detonate the bomb as the Americans closed in, but of course, by then, it had already been dismantled. They tried to fight it out and were cut down.'

'So we were in time after all.'

'Yes, Mr. Navarr, but only just. That transport was due to take off the day after your warning came through. If you'd been a day later they would have succeeded.

The damage to American prestige if the world had been led to believe that they had been negligent enough to let one of their H-planes blow up in the air and destroy their own base and hundreds of innocent islanders, would have been drastic. It might have swayed many of the distrustful races in Asia and Africa into turning to communism. The possible repercussions to such a story are beyond definition, they might have changed the course of history.'

Navarr picked up the half-empty Scotch and soda from the small table by his elbow and swallowed it carefully. 'Well, what happens now?'

'Nothing.' The Consul looked uncomfortable. 'The whole matter has been hushed up. The men who plotted the schemes are dead, so there can be no trial. And to accuse the communists of sponsoring Voron and his organisation would only lead to them denying it. We know Voron was in their pay, but we cannot prove it, and that is what we would be challenged to do. That way we should only lose face. You see, in a propaganda war we must inevitably lose — we have scruples about telling only the truth.'

'So it's all censored?' Navarr's tone was hard.

'I'm afraid so. And I'm afraid too, Mr. Navarr, that I must ask you to say nothing. It would make a great story for the Trans-Continental News Agency, but it's one that must never be printed.'

He leaned forward in his chair and his features were apologetic and ill at ease. 'I'm afraid that all I can offer you both is a heart-felt, but unofficial, thank you. I hope you can understand that this must never become public. To make accusations that we cannot prove would be disastrous.'

Navarr said slowly: 'I understand.' Then he glanced at Lorretta and suddenly smiled. 'Hell, we didn't take that little stroll just for the publicity, did we?'

She laughed. 'I just went for the company.'

The Consul looked relieved. 'I'm so glad you both retained your sense of humour, anyway. He reached out his hand. 'Thank you, Mr. Navarr.'

Navarr took the hand and gripped it. 'Don't worry, the story I'll tell my paper won't mention Voron, or the fact that we were shot down. I'll make it a simple case of a plane crashing from engine failure — it'll still make a good story.'

The Consul turned to Lorretta and shook her hand formally.

'Thank you too, Miss Valoise,' he said. 'If there's anything at all I can do for either of you, don't hesitate to let me know.'

Navarr said quietly: 'I don't think there's anything.'

* * *

Outside the sun was shining, burning down from a clear blue sky. The street was hot and dusty, and filled with hurrying traffic. Fast automobiles, and swerving bicycles flashed past. Men and women shouted and yelled above the roar of the engines, children screamed, a dry wind blew a sheet of old newspaper along the gutter. Navarr and Lorretta walked along the pavement, and then stopped.

Navarr smiled suddenly. 'Isn't life crazy?' he said. 'I live through the biggest story of my career — and then they censor it.'

'It's crazy all right.' Lorretta's eyes were serious. 'We say nothing at all about Schelde, and it doesn't matter anyway. Still — I'm glad we never mentioned him. It might have got back to the other side somehow.'

'I doubt it. But it's something we'll never tell, anyway.' Navarr grinned. 'I liked the solemnity over that unofficial thank you. We had him really uncomfortable, wondering how to put it over.'

She laughed, her eyes twinkling, and the sun made a sea of bronze fire out of the long hair that spilled over her shoulders.

'Who cares about thank-yous? I got a lot more than that out of it.' She locked her arms around his waist suddenly, and kissed him lightly on the mouth. 'I've got you.'

He closed his hands over her shoulders and let the rich silk of her hair flow over them as he spread his fingers under her chin to cup her face upwards. They made a little island in the sea of passers-by. He said quietly: 'You've still got the worst of the bargain.' He felt the gentle motion of her breasts as she pressed closer against him, felt her arms locking tighter around his waist. Her eyes were exceptionally blue and alive; her soft red lips were slightly parted and only inches from his own. He went on softly:

'Do you remember what I told you once, back in the jungle? About taking you out and then making love to you?'

She smiled. 'I said I'd like it. I still would, Steve.'

Their mouths closed and, in the brief seconds before that lingering contact, he murmured:

'I'm going to go one better than just making love to you — I'm going to marry you first.'

Other titles in the
Linford Mystery Library

A LANCE FOR THE DEVIL
Robert Charles

The funeral service of Pope Paul VI was to be held in the great plaza before St. Peter's Cathedral in Rome, and was to be the scene of the most monstrous mass assassination of political leaders the world had ever known. Only Counter-Terror could prevent it.

IN THAT RICH EARTH
Alan Sewart

How long does it take for a human body to decay until only the bones remain? When Detective Sergeant Harry Chamberlane received news of a body, he raised exactly that question. But whose was the body? Who was to blame for the death and in what circumstances?

MURDER AS USUAL
Hugh Pentecost

A psychotic girl shot and killed Mac Crenshaw, who had come to the New England town with the advance party for Senator Farraday. Private detective David Cotter agreed that the girl was probably just a pawn in a complex game — but who had sent her on the assignment?

THE MARGIN
Ian Stuart

It is rumoured that Walkers Brewery has been selling arms to the South African army, and Graham Lorimer is asked to investigate. He meets the beautiful Shelley van Rynveld, who is dedicated to ending apartheid. When a Walkers employee is killed in a hit-and-run accident, his wife tells Graham that he's been seeing Shelly van Rynveld . . .

TOO LATE FOR THE FUNERAL
Roger Ormerod

Carol Turner, seventeen, and a mystery, is very close to a murder, and she has in her possession a weapon that could prove a number of things. But it is Elsa Mallin who suffers most before the truth of Carol Turner releases her.

NIGHT OF THE FAIR
Jay Baker

The gun was the last of the things for which Harry Judd had fought and now it was in the hands of his worst enemy, aimed at the boy he had tried to help. This was the night in which the past had to be faced again and finally understood.

MR CRUMBLESTONE'S EDEN

Henry Crumblestone was a quiet little man who would never knowingly have harmed another, and it was a dreadful twist of irony that caused him to kill in defence of a dream . . .

PAY-OFF IN SWITZERLAND
Bill Knox

'Hot' British currency was being smuggled to Switzerland to be laundered, hidden in a safari-style convoy heading across Europe. Jonathan Gaunt, external auditor for the Queen's and Lord Treasurer's Remembrancer, went along with the safari, posing as a tourist, to get any lead he could. But sudden death trailed the convoy every kilometer to Lake Geneva.

SALVAGE JOB
Bill Knox

A storm has left the oil tanker S.S. *Craig Michael* stranded and almost blocking the only channel to the bay at Cabo Esco. Sent to investigate, marine insurance inspector Laird discovers that the Portuguese bay is hiding a powder keg of international proportions.

BOMB SCARE — FLIGHT 147
Peter Chambers

Smog delayed Flight 147, and so prevented a bomb exploding in mid-air. Walter Keane found that during the crisis he had been robbed of his jewel bag, and Mark Preston was hired to locate it without involving the police. When a murder was committed, Preston knew the stake had grown.

STAMBOUL INTRIGUE
Robert Charles

Greece and Turkey were on the brink of war, and the conflict could spell the beginning of the end for the Western defence pact of N.A.T.O. When the rumour of a plot to speed this possibility reached Counter-espionage in Whitehall, Simon Larren and Adrian Cleyton were despatched to Turkey . . .